COPYRIGHT

REVIEWS

He Completes Me by Cardeno C.: This story is a true "happily ever after"... If you're looking for a sweet, dependable love story that doesn't use gimmicks to pace through the plot, check out He Completes Me.

Home Again by Cardeno C.: It was a hell of a ride. I adored this story and am so glad that I read it. Thank you, Cardeno, for giving me another story to love and re-read.

Love at First Sight by Cardeno C.: I enjoy the sense of family in this story. ... This story is about dreaming and how those dreams change as life happens around us. It's about the decisions we make and how they shape our future. It's a story of struggle and fear that leads to beauty and happiness. This is a story of hope and wonder and of unconditional, unwavering love and loyalty. And I shall not forget to speak of the humor. Not only is this story sweet and dramatic, but it has it's laugh-out-loud moments. ... I love these guys. I love the fictional world that this author has created with this series. And I adore this sweet, sweet story.

The One Who Saves Me by Cardeno C.: I still have that happy feeling inside, the same every Cardeno C. book leaves me with...I can't have enough of Cardeno's books.

Walk With Me by Cardeno C.: I've found that the thing I like best about Cardeno C.'s stories is that the couples easily connect and have wonderful chemistry....This book touched me. I'm not sure if it was the sweet friendship, the sense that these two were meant for each other or the fact that their families and friends were so supportive and loving, but I was all in almost from the moment I read the first page.

— Fiction Vixen

Where He Ends and I Begin by Cardeno C.: I think after reading this story it would be hard for anyone not to believe in true love, and that there one person made just for you to love.

— Two Lips Reviews

DEDICATION

To Crissy Morris with love.

CHAPTER ONE

I'M NOT gay. I'm not gay. I'm not gay.

I know you're thinking that's a weird chant for a straight guy to have as his mantra. But I figure maybe if I think it over and over again, it'll actually be true. I mean, I don't look gay or anything. I'm six feet three inches tall, muscular, and have broad shoulders. That's not small or girly. And I'm athletic. I played varsity sports all through high school, intramurals in college, and I still play in a men's baseball league. I have a deep, strong voice. No lisp in sight. Plus, women like me. I always have a girlfriend. *Always.*

So I'm not gay, right? There must be some other logical explanation for why I'm standing in the bathroom with my hard dick in my hand fantasizing about the new guy at work. For the third time today. And it isn't even lunchtime yet.

Or maybe being gay has nothing to do with all those stereotypes. Maybe being gay just means that no matter how much I wish I could, I'll never react to any woman in the heart-pounding, sweat-inducing, breath-stealing, dick-filling way I react when Micah Trains so much as runs his fingers through his close-cut brown hair.

Shit. Shit. Shit. Maybe I really am gay.

"Ben, are you in here?"

I quickly stuffed my dick back into my pants.

"Yeah. Be out in a sec."

My voice sounded sort of breathless, and I wondered whether it was noticeable to anyone other than me. My hands were shaking when I got to the sink and turned the handle. I know, I know. It's pathetic.

Okay, stop acting like a teenager whose mom just caught him wanking. Nobody knows what you were doing in here. And even if they suspect, they can't know who you were thinking about, so calm down and act normal.

But I knew it wasn't normal to give myself a pep talk in the bathroom while a work colleague was standing at the door waiting for me. I also knew it wasn't normal to think what I had been thinking about the new lawyer in the office. It had to stop. The fantasies, the daydreams, the images. Okay, those were all the same thing, but they had to stop.

I pulled a couple of paper towels from the dispenser and dried my hands slowly. When I was sure my pants were lying flat, all evidence of my earlier arousal hidden away, I walked to the door. Tucker Jones, one of the associates in my practice group, was waiting for me, and I instinctively averted my eyes and walked right past him.

"What's going on, Tucker? You need something?"

I heard him sigh from behind me and knew he noticed that I hadn't looked him in the eye. Again. I realized the guy probably thought I was mental because I always acted sketchy around him, but I didn't see an alternative. I was worried that if I said too much or got to know him too well, he would figure it out.

You see, Tucker's gay. And my brother, Noah, says he can tell when other guys are gay. My taller-than-me, stronger-than-me, more-athletic-than-me, hell, more-masculine-than-me brother, who's as queer as a three-dollar bill and thinks nothing of shouting it from the rooftop. While he's holding hands with my old roommate. Even if everyone can see them.

Funny, I hadn't thought of Clark as my roommate for a long time. Not since I started spending time with him and Noah after being estranged from them for years. Seeing Clark and Noah as a couple changed Clark's status, in my mind, from being my old friend to being my brother's boyfriend. Or is it partner?

Whatever they call one another, there can be no doubt about who they are to each other. One look at the way they gaze at one another, take care of each other, and a blind man would know they're in love. Ten years. That's how long Noah and Clark have been together. Longer if you count the years they spent as friends, biding their time until Noah finished high school.

And I had spent those same years wondering why I couldn't suppress the urge to see Clark naked, touch him, taste him. No matter how many women I dated or even slept with in my life, I never could suppress that urge. Nothing worked. Well, that is until I started spending time with him and my brother. As soon as I did that, it became very clear to me that Clark and Noah were the real deal. I didn't stand a chance, and hell, I didn't even want a chance anymore. Who would want to get in the way of that kind of connection?

So the naked Clark fantasies stopped, and I thought maybe I would be okay. Maybe I would finally be able to make something with a woman last longer than, as Noah so eloquently once put it, a tube of toothpaste. (Just between you and me, that was a generous description, because my tube of Crest has been with me longer than any girlfriend, even without counting the thing where you roll it into a tight little circle to get every last ounce of paste out of it.)

But then Micah Trains walked into the office, wearing a crisp white dress shirt, red and blue striped tie, pressed chinos, and a navy blazer, and I was lost. Completely and totally lost. My old Clark fantasies had nothing on what Micah inspired in my mind. Hence the ridiculously frequent masturbation sessions that barely took the edge off my need.

Anyway, since Tucker Jones, the associate who'd been waiting for me outside the bathroom, was gay, I figured he might be able to do the same thing as Noah with that gaydar, and then he would figure it out about me. I mean, probably not, because I acted perfectly normal. But I didn't see any need to test fate, so I had made it a point to avoid Tucker as much as possible.

"I have a conference call scheduled with a new client in a few minutes." Tucker sounded frustrated. "Randy said he'd sit in on it with me, but his meeting's running late, so he won't be able to make it."

Tucker followed me to my office. I sat down at my desk and shuffled some papers around, pretending like I had something to do, while he shifted from foot to foot. I could tell, because I wouldn't let my eyes go any higher than the man's knees. I didn't say anything, so he kept talking.

"I'd take it on my own, but it's a big client and a pretty complicated deal, and I'd feel a lot more comfortable if a partner was involved too. So can you do it? It shouldn't take too much of your time, and it's all billable."

I didn't see any way out of it, so I forced myself to nod and look up at him. "Sure. I'm happy to help out with the call. Should we do it in your office or mine?"

I blushed as soon as the words left my mouth. Did it sound like I was propositioning him? It wasn't my intention. I mean, Tucker Jones was a good-looking guy, but he had a serious boyfriend, and besides, he wasn't my type. I preferred somebody older than me, not younger. Somebody with a lot of confidence and a big presence. Somebody a little rough around the edges. Somebody like...women. I preferred women.

Yeah, right. Are you buying that? Because it was getting harder and harder to convince myself that it could ever be true.

I WAS working late on Friday, not because there was something time-sensitive that I had to get out, but because I didn't have anything else to do. My girlfriend had tried to get me to go to a dinner party at her friend's house, but I had politely declined. It had been a long week, and the last thing I wanted was the stress of being "on" all night.

I decided to get a soda and then put the finishing touches on a purchase and sale agreement. As I walked down the hallway, my mind was completely focused on indemnity clauses and whether mandatory arbitration made sense in the context of the particular deal. (Look, I never claimed to be interesting. I'm a corporate lawyer. That's not exactly hanging-from-the-chandeliers type of stuff, but it pays the bills.) Anyway, when I got to the office kitchen and saw the man standing there, all work-related thoughts flew from my head and my blood flowed decidedly south.

Micah Trains was leaning against the counter in front of the microwave, reading a document. His nose was bigger than average and a little crooked, like it had been broken a time or two. His short brown hair came together in a widow's peak in front, probably because the sides were receding a bit, and a beard covered much of his face. His jacket and tie were gone, his shirt was crumpled and rolled up to the elbows, and there were little wrinkles on the sides of his blue eyes because he was squinting in the low light. And every single one of those things added up to make an incredibly sexy package. I hated myself for thinking it, but there it was: Micah Trains was sexy as hell.

I didn't realize that I had stopped moving until Micah looked up from the papers in his hand and locked his steel-blue gaze on me. After that, it was all I could do to stay upright. I felt as if my knees were buckling, and I was getting light-headed.

What was wrong with me? Maybe I was coming down with something, like a cold or the flu. *Or repressed homosexuality.* I could hear my brother's voice in my head, sarcastic tone and all, but I shook it off. I couldn't be gay; it would absolutely devastate my parents. One gay son was bad enough, but two? Well, I might as well call the funeral parlors to see if we could get a group discount rate, because it would kill both of them.

Micah cleared his throat and licked his lips. It was an innocent, subconscious action on his part, but I couldn't take my eyes away from his mouth. What would it be like to have that tongue licking my lips? I hoped the sound of the microwave was loud enough to drown out the groan that reflexively left my body.

"Ben Forman, right?" Micah asked as he walked toward me with his hand outstretched. I couldn't move a muscle. "We met last month when I came in to interview with all the partners, but I think Randy Desai monopolized that particular meeting, so we didn't get to talk much. I've been meaning to come say hello and introduce myself more properly, but between transitioning my files over here, getting to know the new computer system, and preparing for a trial set to start in a couple of months, I've been swamped. So it's taken me a little longer than I'd hoped to make the rounds."

I heard his words. I even understood them. But I still couldn't figure out how to make my mouth work so that I could respond. Micah was bowlegged. I hadn't noticed that before, probably because he had been sitting or standing still every time I had seen him, but now I was fixated on the way he walked. Damn, was that ever hot.

I sighed internally. It had gotten to the point where I was finding the way a man walked attractive. I needed help.

Thankfully, my internal struggle snapped me out of my Micah-induced stupor, and I managed to take his hand and shake it without falling over or drooling. I had graduated Order of the Coif, summa cum laude from a top-ten law school, and I was giving myself an internal pat on the back for accomplishing basic bodily function control. Just great.

"Hi, Micah. Nice to see you again. So you're settling in okay?"

Three sentences, and I got them all out without stammering. Well, not too badly, anyway. I was pretty sure Micah hadn't noticed.

The microwave beeped.

I smiled.

Micah raised one eyebrow, and the side of his mouth tilted up in stomach-flipping grin. "I'm going to need to ask for my hand back so I can get that popcorn out of the microwave."

"Oh, uh, yeah. Sorry."

I let go of his hand and walked over the fridge, keeping my face inside it under the guise of searching for a soda, but I was actually just waiting for the blush to subside. Had I held onto his hand too long? I didn't think so, but then everything seemed to be sort of hazy and moving in slow motion.

"Can I get you a soda, Micah?"

There. That sounded just fine. Even voice, not shaking, complete sentence. Yeah, I know you're impressed.

"That'd be great. Thanks."

I got the drinks out of the fridge and turned back toward Micah, feeling a bit more in control of my body and my emotions. He was sitting at the table, munching on popcorn and making some notes on the document he was reading. It would have been rude not to sit down and talk to him for a little while. He was new to the firm and one of my partners now. I should make an effort to get to know him.

I didn't know why I felt the need to justify my behavior to myself. There was nothing unusual about taking a break at work with another lawyer. Of course, there was definitely something unusual about the way I reacted to Micah Trains.

Okay, fine, maybe I *did* know the reason for the internal justifications.

"So tell me about yourself, Ben. I know you're in the transactional group, that you recently made partner, and that blue's your favorite color, but that's about it."

My jaw dropped. "How do you know my favorite color?"

"Because I've seen you around the office and I noticed that about seventy percent of your shirts are some shade of blue or a close variation, like blue checkers or stripes."

"You're remarkably observant," I said.

He shrugged. "I can be when it matters."

He pushed the popcorn bag toward me. Then he opened his soda, tilted his head back, stretching his long neck, and took a few gulps. I watched his throat work as he swallowed down his beverage.

I wanted him. There was no denying it. My entire body was tight and thrumming with need.

Why couldn't I have that feeling with a woman? I dreaded the nights when I couldn't come up with a decent excuse and I had to go to bed with whatever woman I was dating at the time. I was getting older and it was getting more and more difficult for me to be able to fake an interest, and I was sick of trying.

Maybe I needed to take a break from dating for a little while. Nobody would think anything of it if I was single for a few months. That wasn't a red flag or anything. Lots of guys went for months at a time without a girlfriend.

A piece of popcorn hit my forehead and startled me.

"Earth to Ben." Micah was grinning like a loon.

"Did you just throw popcorn at me?" I tried not to laugh.

The move was so incongruous with Micah Trains's cutthroat litigator reputation. The man was supposed to be type A, a brilliant strategist, and vicious in the court room. And here he was fooling around like a teenager.

"Hey, I had to do something to get your attention."

Oh, he had my attention. That wasn't an issue. The problem was just how much of my attention was fixated on the man. Emphasis on the "man" part of that sentence.

CHAPTER TWO

"ALL RIGHT, you've got my attention and an A for creativity. What can I do for you, Micah?"

A single eyebrow rose again, and this time when Micah's lips curved upward, I could have sworn he was leering more than smiling. I shook off the thought. That was impossible.

Micah Trains was one of the top litigators in Emile City. That wasn't just my personal opinion. He had actually been listed as one of the top fifty litigators in a survey of all state bar members two years running. Considering the fact that he wasn't even forty years old yet, that was quite an achievement. Anyway, the point was that a guy like that couldn't be gay, so there was no way he would leer at me.

"I assume you're not trying to meet a deadline, since business hours are over until Monday morning. Is that right, or do you have some pain in the ass client expecting you to get something done by Saturday morning?" he asked.

I laughed. "I have a lot of pain in the ass clients, but none of them have any pressing deadlines right now."

Micah smiled broadly. He got up from the table and tossed the popcorn bag across the room and into the trash can. Clark and I used to play games like that in high school, and I smiled at the memory. "Two points. Well done," I said.

"Two points? No fuckin' way. That was a three-point shot. Come on, let's go."

I laughed in spite of myself. Hotshot lawyer with a potty mouth. Of course, I found that attractive too. Maybe he could pick his nose or something equally disgusting so I could kick the unwelcome attraction plaguing me. I was following him out of the kitchen before I realized it.

"Wait. Where're we going?"

He just kept walking down the hallway toward his office. It was on the opposite side of the floor from mine. I knew because it had been a stretch for me to keep coming up with excuses to walk by and look at him out of the corner of my eye at least once—okay, fine, three times—a day since he started.

"We're going to dinner. I'm starving and popcorn won't do. Since you don't have a deadline, I figure you can join me."

We had gotten to his office, and he slid into his chair and shut down his computer. Then he picked up his wallet and cell phone and stuffed them into his pocket.

"Do you need to log off?" he asked me.

I didn't remember agreeing to have dinner with him, but I supposed it made sense. We were both working late, it was Friday night... No, actually, it didn't make sense. I had never spontaneously made weekend dinner plans with one of my partners. Well, most of them had families waiting for them at home or plans with friends.

I was pretty sure Micah Trains was single. I didn't know anything about his personal life, but he wasn't wearing a wedding ring, and there weren't any wedding or kid photos in his office. As successful as he was, I figured he was one of those guys who was married to his career. He probably had an ex-wife or two who'd vouch for that.

"Yeah. Give me a minute and I'll meet you at the elevator bank," I said.

I turned around and started walking out of Micah's office and heard his footsteps behind me. I looked over my shoulder. He was right there with his suit jacket and tie draped over his arm.

"I'll walk with you. Give me a chance to see how the other half lives. I've never been to the transactional side of the floor."

"It's nothing exciting," I told him as we walked through the quiet, dark hallways. "Just a mirror image of the litigation side. We tend to have less shouting during the day, but that's about it as far as differences go."

And I should know exactly what was and wasn't different between the litigation and transactional wings, considering my bordering-on-stalking routine visits to his side of the floor, which had not coincidentally started on the day he joined the firm.

When we got to my office, Micah immediately started

looking at the pictures on my credenza. I only had a few: one of my parents all dressed up for a charity event a few years prior, one of the four of us—me, my parents, and my brother—from when I was a kid. And a fairly recent picture that Clark had snapped of me and Noah.

The picture was nothing special. We were just sitting on the couch in his living room wearing jeans and T-shirts. But there were a lot of years when I didn't think I would ever have even that level of relationship with my brother, so I cherished it. Even more so because Clark had not only taken the picture, but he had printed it, framed it, and given it to me. I had made a lot of mistakes over the years when it came to Clark, so that picture felt like forgiveness to me.

"Hey, I know this guy. Noah, right? Noah Forman." Micah paused for a heartbeat, and I saw his eyes flicker as the light bulb went on. "You're Noah Forman's brother?"

I was surprised that Micah knew Noah. They weren't the same age—Noah was twenty-seven, which made him about a decade younger than Micah. And they weren't in the same line of work—Noah owned a kickboxing gym.

"Yeah, I am. How do you know Noah?"

"We have a mutual friend, so I end up running into Noah and his partner, Clark, every so often. They're great guys. Even though your brother can be a little, ehm, intense about Clark."

I laughed at that diplomatic description of Noah's possessive streak when it came to Clark.

"Yeah, he can be pretty intense. But Clark doesn't seem to mind, so…" I shrugged and let the thought trail off. There had been a time when just thinking of my brother and Clark together would have made me angry. I had wanted to save Noah from what I was sure would be a hollow life. I thought if he got away from Clark, he would meet a nice girl, settle down, and be happy. That was how it was supposed to work, right? Well, as it turned out, Noah was settled and very happy already. With Clark. I, on the other hand, had met lots of nice girls, and I was neither settled nor happy.

I had finished shutting down my computer, so I started walking out of my office. I was in front of Micah, which turned out to be a good thing, because it stopped him from seeing me almost swallow my tongue when I heard his next sentence.

"Gay brothers, huh? Have you ever looked into the odds on that? I'd bet it's pretty unusual."

I wanted to deny it. I wanted to tell him that I wasn't like Noah. I wanted to say that I was straight. But I was so busy concentrating on walking and breathing that I couldn't manage to say a word, and then he moved on from the conversation, so the moment passed, and it was too late to correct him.

"How do you feel about Indian? Bombay Palace is pretty good, and it's down the street, so we can walk. I feel like over the past week or so it's finally gotten warm enough that I can go outside even after the sun's gone down."

"Oh, uh, sure. Sounds good."

My head was swimming. Why did Micah think I was gay?

"So did you grow up here in Emile City?" Micah asked as if the world weren't crashing down around us. Actually, the mundane normalness of the question calmed me a little. At least enough to make conversation.

"Yes, I did, in EC North. I still live there, actually."

It helped that we were walking and talking, because I didn't have to look at his face and see what he really thought of me. His voice was perfectly even, like it didn't bother him at all to be walking to dinner with a gay guy. No, not a gay guy, a guy he thought was gay but actually wasn't. Yeah, right.

Anyway, Micah Trains hadn't accidentally tripped into his reputation as a top-notch attorney. He probably had a knack for hiding his real opinions and making people feel comfortable talking. Of course, I wasn't a hostile witness, so there was no reason for him to try to get me to open up. "That's quite a commute every day," he said.

I shrugged. "Just under an hour. It's not terrible. I've thought about getting a place closer to the office, but my parents like having me out there."

There wasn't really anything else to say about it. I owned a pretty basic one-bedroom condo in a nothing-to-write-home-about complex. I didn't love it, but I didn't hate it either, and I could get to my parents' house in less than ten minutes, which was useful because my mother liked having me over for dinner often. Too often, really, but I always went when she asked. I felt like I had to go often enough to count as two sons worth of visits, because Noah refused to grace them with his presence.

"I grew up in LA, and when I moved away, I swore I'd never have to deal with traffic again," Micah said. "My drive is about fifteen minutes during rush hour, less than ten if I'm driving in early or going home late."

"Oh, now you're just being cruel and rubbing my face in it. I'll have to spend this evening's commute thinking of creative payback ideas." I tried to sound menacing, but I think I probably fell a little short. I wasn't the scary type.

Micah just laughed. "All right, pretty boy. Give it your best shot."

DINNER TURNED out to be fun.

We talked about work.

Micah had a few different cases going, but the one taking most of his time had a trial date scheduled for September. I had a few purchase and sale transactions and some corporate formations on my desk.

"The thing I like about corporate work is that we're all striving for the same goal. I mean, I still have to deal with opposing counsel, and we're each trying to get the best terms we can for our clients. But at the end of the day, we both want to get the deal done, so we have a strong incentive to play nice and make things work," I explained.

"It's not always like that with litigation," he said. "People play a lot of games. They try to stretch things out and waste the other guy's time and money. Take when I moved to the firm, for example. One asshole opposing counsel tried to file a motion to remove me from the Jones case saying there was suddenly some conflict, even though we cleared conflicts checks before I came over. It was a total bullshit delay tactic because the trial date's coming up and he thinks if he strings it out further, my guy will settle."

I didn't understand half of that because litigation was completely outside the scope of what I did, but I got the general idea. "So what'd you do? You're still working on the case, right?"

He grabbed some naan, tore off a piece, and popped it in his mouth. "Oh, hell yeah, I'm still on it. I just wrote opposing counsel back and told him to go fuck himself, fuck his mom, fuck his dog, and fuck his mom's dog."

I raised my eyebrows in surprise. "That worked?"

He smirked. "Well, I phrased it more delicately, but the message was the same. And, yeah, it worked. I can be extremely persuasive."

Yeah, I bet. I had a feeling Micah Trains could persuade me to do just about anything. It wouldn't take much, really, just him asking in that sexy-as-hell raspy voice. Damn it, there I went again. My mind was completely out of control.

We talked about family.

Micah had a younger sister who lived in LA, along with his parents. My parents and younger brother all lived in Emile City.

"Are you close with your family?" I asked him.

"Absolutely. I get out there to visit them at least every couple of months or my mother starts calling and leaving progressively more annoying voicemails." He made a funny face and started talking in a high, nasally voice. "Micah, this is your mother, Deborah Stern Trains, calling. I thought I should use my full name in case you've forgotten. After all, I know how busy you are and how many different people you talk to every day. I don't mean to bother you, but I thought you should know that your nephew misses you. I've tried telling him that his uncle is a very important man and very important men don't always have time to call their families, even their only nephew who thinks they hung the moon. But he's only five, so he doesn't understand. Don't worry. I'll keep explaining it to him."

I was laughing so hard by the time he was done with the impression that I had to wipe tears away from the corners of my eyes. "You're exaggerating!" I gasped out.

He shook his head. "I wish. That was practically verbatim. And that's if I don't call for a week. If I go any longer, she'll call again and lay it on even thicker."

He cleared his throat and did the impression voice again. "Micah, this is your mother calling. Again. I just want to let you know that my telephone number hasn't changed and I still live in the same place. I know you must be worried about that because I can't sleep at night for worrying about you. Your father keeps telling me to take an Ambien, but you know how upset my stomach gets when I take pharmaceuticals. Don't worry, I'm used to not getting much sleep. When I was pregnant with you, you kept me up all night. But just in case my body can't take it anymore now that I'm old, please make sure your father doesn't break the bank on the funeral. I'm not the Queen of England. Hopefully, you'll make time to come to my funeral, but I'll understand if you're too busy. I'll talk to your father now, so he'll understand too. We miss you. You can call anytime you're free. I'll stop whatever I'm doing, because I know how valuable your time is and that mine isn't as important."

We talked about religion.

He was Jewish and belonged to a small synagogue that he really liked. I was raised in a nondenominational Christian church, but I only went when my parents asked me to join them.

"I don't know what I believe or if I believe anything." I shrugged. "I don't really give it much thought, I guess."

"It's more of a cultural thing than a God thing for me," he explained. "It's important to me to carry on the traditions. I like the ritual of it, you know? I like knowing that my grandparents and their grandparents all read those same prayers and celebrated those same holidays, and that my niece and nephew and future generations will do the same thing. Whether or not there's a higher power out there, being part of that tradition makes me feel like I'm part of something bigger than myself."

We talked about hobbies.

I was right about his work ethic. It sounded like Micah worked exceptionally long hours. When he had free time, he liked to hike and bike. I told him about the men's baseball league I played with, my fantasy baseball league, and my obsession with Emile City's Major League Baseball team, the Glory.

"So are you a Glory season ticket holder?" he asked.

I shook my head and gulped down some water. The tikka masala was seriously spicy. "I wish. I can't afford to buy an entire season, not that I'd have the time to go to eighty-one games even if I could. And getting into a share with good seats is almost impossible. Once someone gets a lock on those, he has to move away or die before he'll give them up."

"Yeah, that's true. Their luck needs to turn around soon, though, or that might change. If the Glory are gonna win a game, those boys need to learn how to close it out."

WHEN THE bill came, I reached for my wallet, but Micah waved me off, put his credit card on the tray, and handed it to the waiter.

"You don't have to do that, Micah. We can split it."

"Nope. I invited you to dinner, so it's my treat."

His voice was softer than it had been all night. He was smiling, and there was something in his eyes that tugged at my chest. I had the strangest feeling at that moment that I was on a date instead of having a casual dinner with a work colleague.

I knew it wasn't true. I knew that wasn't how Micah saw the evening. But my deranged mind couldn't stop itself from running on that track, and I hated myself for it.

CHAPTER THREE

I WAS quiet as we walked back to the firm's parking garage after dinner.

Why did my brain have to misinterpret everything? Why couldn't I spend time with a man I found attractive without having to twist the evening into something dirty and wrong? And how could I make myself stop finding Micah, or any other man, attractive?

"Do you have any exciting plans for the weekend?" Micah asked, interrupting my mental anguish.

I forced myself to keep my voice even as I answered. The last thing I needed was for the hotshot new lawyer in the office to realize that I was just a step or two away from a complete breakdown. "Not really. I'll probably get some work done and go visit my parents tomorrow. Sunday, I'm parking my butt in front of the TV and watching the Glory game. I hope it'll be exciting and not another heartbreaker in the last couple of innings."

I left out the date I had planned with my girlfriend the following evening. It seemed wrong, for some reason, to talk to Micah about her. Not that it mattered, because if my track record stayed consistent, Jill and I would break up within a week. And a month after that, I would need to buy a new tube of toothpaste.

Micah was parked right by the parking garage entrance. When we got to his car, he paused and turned to me. We were suddenly standing so close I could feel his breath on my face and his heat radiating against my skin. And just like that, my dick thickened and lengthened in my pants.

I had to get out of there before Micah realized how he affected me. I turned on my heel and started speed walking toward the stairs, talking to Micah over my shoulder as I went. "Thanks for dinner, Micah. I'll see you on Monday."

I was walking so fast that I had already reached the stairwell door by the time he was able to answer.

"Hey, Ben."

I stopped and took a deep breath before I turned around. At that distance and with the dim light in the garage, he wouldn't be able to see my arousal.

When I was facing him, he kept talking. "I had a great time tonight. Thanks for agreeing to go out with me."

I couldn't say anything in response. My mind was, once again, misinterpreting every word and trying to convince me that I had just gone on a date with the sexiest, smartest, funniest man I had ever met. I raised my hand in a silent goodbye and walked into the stairwell.

THE NEXT evening, I was getting ready for my date with Jill when my phone beeped, telling me I had received a text. I wasn't surprised or disappointed when I picked it up and read the message from Jill: "*Ben, I don't think it's working out. I hope we can stay friends. I'll see you around.*"

You might think it was rude of her to break up with me via text, but we had been together less than two weeks. Besides, I preferred the text to having an in-person conversation. At least now I didn't have to suffer through the date with a smile on my face, wondering the entire time how I could get out of spending the night at her place.

I thought about calling my friends to see what they were doing that night, but what would be the point? We would probably end up hitting the bars and picking up women. I was so damn tired of juggling everything, of constantly trying to be *that* guy. You know the one—the good son, the fun friend, the desirable boyfriend. The guy my parents and everyone else expected me to be. Frankly, I was just plain tired.

And I couldn't stop thinking about Micah Trains. He had been unexpectedly funny at dinner the previous night. I had known from his reputation that the man was intelligent and cutthroat. But I hadn't expected him to be so nice, to seemingly adore his family and talk in a funny voice in the middle of a restaurant doing impressions of his mother, to ask me questions about myself and patiently listen to the answers as if he really cared to know those kinds of details about my life.

Plus, there was the chemistry. Yes, it was one-sided. I didn't lie to myself and pretend otherwise. But it was still there. The constant feeling of warmth in my belly when I was with him. The way the tea lights on the table made his blue eyes sparkle whenever he looked at me, which was almost constantly. The time we both reached for the naan and our hands touched—I swear it was like a spark started in my fingers and slithered through my body until it settled in my groin, creating an instant erection.

I sat down on my couch and, just for a moment, dropped my defenses and shut out the guilt that seemed to be my constant companion. I let myself think about Micah Trains. I thought about his smile and the way he walked. I thought about his funny stories and the times when his voice seemed to get almost tender as he spoke to me. I thought about how close our bodies had been at the end of the night.

I shivered and sighed. It felt so incredibly good to enjoy someone that much, to really want someone. The feelings were so strong, so intense, that I didn't know how I would be able to avoid them. No, it was more than that. I didn't *want* to avoid them. I wanted to be able to feel that way. It was so much better than the constant anxiety and self-directed anger that made me feel sick inside most days.

I thought about what would happen if I let myself feel that way all the time, if I stopped trying to be the guy my parents needed me to be. *My parents*. It would ruin my mother if I said I was... I couldn't even let myself think the word.

No, it was enough with Noah. It had always been enough with Noah. My brother had such a large presence that even though he was almost four years younger, he had dominated the house. My parents had been so busy throughout our childhood, trying to keep Noah calm and safe and just generally in control that there hadn't been any room for me to be anything other than perfect.

Then, when Noah told us about his relationship with Clark, things went from bad to worse. At first, my parents blamed me for bringing Clark into our lives. He was my friend, after all.

They were right and I knew it. I felt like I had set Noah up for failure, especially because I knew how enticing Clark could be. By that point in time, I had spent close to a decade trying to squash my own feelings for my friend.

And my brother, staying consistent with his life-long pattern, didn't give any of us an inch to adjust. He insisted that Clark would be joining him at every family gathering or he wouldn't come at all. He became angry and belligerent if any of us asked him to reconsider and try to date women. And that was really saying something, considering the fact that my brother was already angry and belligerent before that altercation.

Noah was so damn young at the time, just twenty-two, and he had been living with Clark since he was eighteen, supposedly as roommates. We were sure some distance from Clark would give him a different perspective. Well, my parents were sure, anyway. Distance from Clark hadn't done a thing to change my perspective with regard to my own feelings for the man, so I wasn't completely sure it would work for Noah. But I wanted him to try. I didn't want my younger brother to suffer through the miserable life I was leading, constantly being plagued by desires and thoughts I knew were wrong.

The irony of it all was that, as it turned out, Noah hadn't been suffering. He was happy with his life, happy living with Clark. And he felt no shame about admitting who he was to anyone who asked and even people who didn't.

I felt equal parts envy and resentment toward my brother. He hadn't ever asked permission for anything. He had just taken what he wanted, done what he wanted, and the rest of us had been stuck picking up the pieces. My parents were still devastated that their youngest son was living a gay lifestyle, and I was still trying to deal with that, still trying to mend the bridge between them and Noah, still hoping that our family could overcome the huge rift that had been formed when he came out. Or, to be more accurate, the rift that had always been there between my brother and my parents.

The bottom line was there simply wasn't room in our family for me to add to the drama and the chaos. I had to be the son my parents expected, because if I wasn't, there would be nobody else left to play that role.

Sitting all alone in my living room thinking about my family, or even worse, thinking about myself, was too much. I felt like I was suffocating, and I needed to get some air. My condo had windows, but no balcony and certainly no yard, so I snatched my keys from the bowl by the door and headed out for a drive. I didn't have a particular destination in mind. I was just driving and thinking, then trying to clear my head with limited success and thinking again.

Before I knew it, I found myself in EC West, turning down my brother's street. I liked his neighborhood so much better than mine. The houses were older and unique, not cookie-cutter McMansions, like where my parents lived, or nondescript condo complexes, like where I lived. I had thought about moving to EC West more than once. It was close to work, close to Noah and Clark, and far away from my parents. But it was far away from my parents. Don't worry, the contradiction in those last two thoughts didn't escape my notice.

I loved my parents. I wanted them to be happy. I wanted them to be proud of me. But sometimes, I wondered if it would ever be possible for me to be happy and proud of myself.

Shaking off those types of thoughts had become so customary that I usually didn't even have to think about it. But as I sat in front of my brother's adorable house and inhaled the scent from the flowers he and Clark had planted in the front yard, I found myself struggling to paste on my standard happy grin. I closed my eyes and breathed deeply.

Everything was fine. I had just been tested more than usual the previous night. But I would find a way to overcome my attraction to Micah Trains. And, if not overcome it, then bury it deep enough that nobody would know. And really, don't you think that's the same thing?

I decided to get out of my car and go say hello to Noah and Clark. My relationship with Clark had improved substantially over the previous four months, which had helped alleviate a sick feeling I'd had since our falling out years earlier. Things were still a little tense with Noah, but then again, things had always been a little tense with Noah, so that was nothing new.

I rang the doorbell and was surprised when my brother's friend opened the door. He was my height, with intentionally disheveled hair that was bleached or dyed or something, resulting in a blond-streaked look. He had long sideburns and all sorts of piercings in both ears, plus one on his eyebrow.

"Oh, sorry, I didn't realize Noah and Clark had company. I should have called first," I said.

"Hey, no worries, man. Come on in." He stepped aside and then held his hand out. "I'm Andrew. We met a couple of months ago." He had some ink on his forearm, but it was just peeking out from under the long-sleeved henley he wore, so I couldn't see the details.

I took his hand and shook it. "I remember. Nice to see

you again, Andrew. I'm sorry to interrupt your evening."

"Seriously, it's not a problem. There's plenty of food. Come on out back."

My mother would have been mortified if she had known that I had come to someone's home uninvited and unannounced and interrupted a dinner party. Oh, and I was empty-handed, not even a bottle of wine to share. Social niceties were very important in my family, and I was probably violating any number of rules. Well, Noah never seemed to care about any of that stuff, and it was his house and his dinner party, so I thought it was probably okay.

We had just stepped out of the french doors into the backyard when Clark saw us. He jogged over to me and clasped my shoulder, giving it a squeeze. "Hi! I'm so glad you're here." He was smiling and his voice sounded genuinely pleased. "I wasn't sure if Noah had decided to... Ehm, what can I get you to eat? We have plenty left—burgers and dogs, a couple of different salads. What are you in the mood for?"

I decided not to apologize for crashing their party, because based on Clark's comment, I was fairly sure he thought Noah had invited me. If I knew Clark and Noah, which I did, I would guess that Clark had suggested including me on the guest list and Noah had refused.

"I'm not all that hungry, Clark. But I'd love a bottle of water."

"Coming right up. Make yourself at home. I think you've met most of the people here."

I looked around the backyard. There were probably about a dozen people there, and most of them looked familiar. I had joined Clark and Noah for dinner or breakfast or a pickup ball game many times over the past few months, and their friends had been included much of the time. I didn't know any of them well, but certainly enough to make small talk. Hey, it was better than spending the night all alone in my condo.

I said hello to some guys I recognized, chatted about the Glory's season and the weather, and then I spotted my brother. He looked surprised to see me but not pissed off. I took that as a win and walked over to him, reaching for a hug as soon as I was close enough. Noah didn't pull away. Hey, I was on a roll.

"Nice to see you. Did Clark invite you?"

Right to the point. Yup, that was Noah.

"No, he didn't. I was just stopping by to say hello. But he thinks you invited me, and he was pretty happy about that. Don't worry, I won't tell him that I'm just here coincidentally."

Noah sighed. "I don't lie to Clark, Ben. Not about anything. Not ever."

No, of course not. They were the perfect couple. All sunshine and roses and rainbows and unicorns. At least when I wasn't butting in and messing things up for them. I suddenly felt drop-dead tired again. I rubbed my eyes with the palm of my hand. "I didn't mean anything by that, Noah.

Sorry. Do you want me to leave?"

"Of course not. I want you to stay. You're always welcome here, Ben." He smirked. "And I'm saying that without Clark here elbowing my ribs. Look, I didn't invite you because I thought you'd be uncomfortable. That's all. But everyone's gonna be taking off soon anyway, so it should be fine."

"Uncomfortable?" I furrowed my brow. "Why?"

"Because of the rest of the guests, Ben. Come on, you're still riding the denial train, and I didn't think you'd want to make a pit stop here in honestyville."

I knew Noah was referring to his recurring accusation that I was gay. There was no point in my denying it. I had already been down that path with Noah, and he wasn't going to buy what I was selling. My brother was much smarter than his brutish appearance implied.

"Thanks for the reminder of how little you think of me, Noah, but I'm perfectly comfortable here."

Okay, so it was a lie. But it wasn't because I was at Noah's house. It seemed like I wasn't comfortable anywhere anymore. Not even in my own skin.

CHAPTER FOUR

I CHATTED with Noah for a little while, but then a few of his guests were leaving, so he went to see them out. I saw a blonde woman standing on the side patio, and I walked over to her out of habit. That was my pattern—find a woman, start dating her, break up, find another woman right away, start dating her, rinse and repeat ad nauseam.

"Hi, I'm Ben Forman." I introduced myself to the blonde woman.

She was holding a can of beer and her hand was wet, so she wiped it on her jeans before reaching it out to me. "I'm Kelsey. Your last name is Forman, huh? Are you Noah's brother?"

I nodded. "Sure am. How do you know Clark and Noah?"

She drank some of her beer before answering. "My girlfriend teaches a couple of classes at Noah's gym."

Well that was unexpected. "Girlfriend? You mean you're, umm, you're…."

Keeping a girlfriend wasn't my forte, but landing one had never been an issue, so knowing I had just struck out with Kelsey had caught me off guard. Sure, I had decided to give myself a reprieve from dating, but a long-standing habit was hard to break, and I had already slated Kelsey as my next future ex-girlfriend. See, I can joke about the ridiculousness that is my life.

"A lesbian. Three syllables, I think you can manage them. I can't imagine that comes as a total shock. I mean, what exactly says straight to you about this hairstyle?" she asked as she waved her hand around her almost military-style buzz cut.

My brother's comment about me being uncomfortable because of the other guests finally sank in. I darted my eyes around the backyard and saw things in a different light.

Andrew, the punk guy who'd let me in, had his arm slung over a slender guy's shoulders. David, a man with black hair and rippling muscles whom I had met when Noah and I went out for drinks one night, was standing behind another dark-haired guy with his arms wrapped around the guy's chest. Aaron, the blond veterinarian who took care of Noah's new puppy, was sitting on one of the teak armchairs with a little man curled in his lap.

Okay, all those guys were paired up with each other. It was funny. To hear my parents describe it, they were terrified about Noah being gay because of the promiscuous lifestyle, the accompanying drug use, and the social isolation associated with homosexuality. But here I was, looking at my brother's tight-knit group of friends, and they were all just hanging out, seemingly sober and very clearly in established relationships. The difference between the reality I was witnessing and the nightmare stories I had always heard confused me.

"I think I may be the only straight person here," I said dumbly.

"Oh, honey, no you're not," she replied, shaking her head before taking a swig of her beer.

"I'm not? Who else is straight?"

"Not what I meant," she said as she walked away across the yard.

It took a full minute for the meaning of her comment to register, and when it did, I felt the blood drain from my face and my stomach roll over. I collapsed into one of the chairs on Noah's patio.

Did she think I was gay? Why? I was acting perfectly normal.

Then it hit me. My brother must have told her about his suspicions. I wondered whether he told everyone that his brother was gay. Maybe that was how Micah Trains knew. Well, not *knew*, but *thought*. Whatever, you get the point.

Micah said he and Noah had a mutual friend, so if Noah was going around telling his friends about me, it might've gotten back to Micah. And if Micah knew—*thought*—that I was gay, I wondered who else had heard Noah's rumor and believed it.

"There you are."

I looked up and saw Clark standing next to me.

"We wondered where you'd gone. Your car is still out front, but we couldn't find you."

I looked toward the backyard and saw that it was empty. I had no idea how long I had been sitting at the side of the house in the near dark, trapped in my own thoughts. "Did everyone go inside?" I asked.

Clark shook his head. "No, they all went home. It's getting kind of late, and we started the barbeque pretty early, so..." Clark tilted his head to the side and appraised me carefully. Even though we had drifted apart, there was a time when we had been really close, and Clark could still read me pretty well. "What's going on, Ben? Are you okay?"

I knew he was trying to be nice, but I didn't feel like hearing it. Noah had no right to talk about me to the world, and I was pissed as hell. "Where's my brother?"

Apprehension and concern etched over Clark's handsome face. "Look, Ben, whatever it is that's gotten you worked up, you need to calm down before you talk to Noah. There's no reason to start something."

Of course, *I* had to be the one to calm down. I always had to be the one to calm down, or let it go, or make some other accommodation for my emotionally unstable brother. I was sick of it. "Where is he, Clark?"

Glaring at Clark, with my teeth gritted so tightly my jaw hurt, I was probably as mad as he'd ever seen me.

His shoulders slumped and he sighed resignedly before pointing toward the french doors. "He's inside."

I started storming toward the door, but Clark clutched my arm. "Please, Ben. Things have gotten so much better between us lately. I don't want us to move backward, and I know you don't either."

I noticed that he hadn't mentioned my brother. Of course not. Noah didn't give a shit about me. He never had. I had always been the one who'd put in all the work to try to maintain any type of relationship with my brother.

"Noah!" I shouted his name before I'd even had a chance to open the door. "Noah, where are you?"

"I'm in here, Ben." His voice was coming from the bedroom, so I made my way back there. "Damn, boy. Where's the fire?"

Noah's sarcasm was the last thing I needed at that moment.

"I don't appreciate you telling all your friends that you think I'm…that you think I'm…"

"That I think you're the only lawyer in Emile City who can't complete a sentence?" Noah drawled.

"Shove it, Noah. I don't appreciate you telling people that you think I'm gay."

There. I said it.

"I assure you, Ben, I've told my friends no such thing."

"Don't lie to me. I know you told them." I didn't want to say anything about Micah Trains, but Kelsey's comment was enough proof that I knew the truth. "Your friend Kelsey told me."

Noah sat on the bed, leaned back on his elbows, and crossed his legs at his ankles. "Kelsey told you that I said you're gay?"

I hated how calm he sounded and that little smirk he wore on his face. "No, she didn't say it like that. But she thinks I'm gay. Why else would she think that? It's not like I act gay or anything."

Noah's lips tightened and his nostrils flared. He sat up straight. "You don't *act* gay?"

"What? I don't. You know I don't. Nobody can tell. I act completely straight."

He laughed when I said that. My life was falling apart and Noah was laughing at me. Typical.

"You check out other guys and lust after them. Newsflash for you, Ben, straight guys don't *act* that way."

I couldn't respond to that accusation. It was true, and I was too worn out to argue about it. I collapsed on the bed next to him. "That doesn't give you the right to talk about me to other people, Noah."

"Don't flatter yourself, Ben. You're not on my mind enough to warrant a conversation to my friends about your pathetic life in the closet. Or anything else about you, for that matter."

"Noah!" Clark's indignant voice interrupted our conversation. He was the only person alive who could get away with using that tone with Noah without walking away with a limp or a bloody nose. "Please don't say things like that, sweetheart. There's no reason to be cruel."

"Yeah? Well, I think there's a reason. I'm sick and tired of biting my tongue while he embarrasses himself by parading around all those beards he calls girlfriends." Noah turned from Clark to me. "Haven't you had enough, Ben? I don't understand why you keep hiding who you are."

"You don't understand what it's like for me," I spat out, hoping the wetness in my eyes wasn't visible.

"I understand perfectly, Ben. I did it, didn't I? I came out. And I was a hell of a lot younger than you at the time."

I rolled my eyes. "Of course *you* did, Noah. But things aren't as easy for me."

He shot off the bed and clenched his fists. Clark walked over and stood next to him, keeping a hand on his shoulder.

"Easy?" Noah said incredulously. "You have no idea what I went through, Ben."

I hadn't meant to get into this, but now that we were talking about it, no way was I backing down. "I have *every* idea what you went through!" I shouted. "I grew up in that same house, remember?"

Noah opened his mouth to respond but then closed it. For the first time in my life, I had managed to shut my brother up. The angry heat left his eyes, and it was replaced by something else. Understanding, maybe? I wasn't sure.

It hadn't been easy in our house. It wasn't that our parents didn't love us, because they did. And money wasn't an issue—we were pretty well off. But there had always been comments, clear indications of disapproval related to anybody different, especially gay people. Of course, when Noah came out, what had been a lifetime of snide remarks and mutters of disapproval about other people had turned into utter devastation about Noah himself and the reflection his choice had on our entire family.

"I didn't tell my friends that you're gay. I wouldn't do that. I might not understand why you don't just come out. I might not approve. But I'd never out you against your will." His voice was quiet and sincere.

I believed him. I wondered once again why Micah thought I was gay. Maybe it was because I had never been married. That could be considered a red flag once a guy was in his thirties. I was already thirty-one.

I felt like I was going to throw up. I couldn't do that, couldn't marry a woman. Dating was one thing, but marriage…that meant something. I just couldn't.

I was sitting on Noah and Clark's bed, my forearms resting on my knees and my head turned toward the hardwood floors.

"Do you ever wish you were different? You know, that you were straight?" I asked them.

After I posed the question, I looked up at the two of them. They were standing next to each other, sides pressed together. Clark had both arms wrapped around Noah's waist, and Noah had his arm draped possessively over Clark's shoulder.

They didn't need to say a word. I already knew the answer. They were at peace and happy. So happy. I wanted to feel that way more than anything.

I WENT for a long run the next morning, hoping to loosen my tight muscles and release some stress. My phone was ringing when I walked back into my condo. It looked like the main switchboard number from my office. Strange. It was Sunday.

"Hello."

"All right! The cell phone list on the firm directory is updated. Hi, Ben. This is Micah."

I couldn't hold back the smile that immediately took over my face. Just the sound of his deep, gravelly voice did that to me. I was so completely screwed. "Hi, Micah. What's up?"

There was a husky little laugh, and then he cleared his throat and answered. "I have tickets to this afternoon's Glory game. Fourth row up, behind home plate. You interested in joining me?"

"Seriously?" Was I squeaking? "Ehm, yeah, I mean, yes, I'd love to come with you."

Oh, God. I did *not* just say that. The man probably thought I was a complete pervert. No, he probably thought it was a normal comment. I actually *was* a complete pervert, which was why my mind had twisted it into something dirty. My entire face was on fire. Thank goodness we were on the phone and Micah couldn't see me.

"Great. Game starts at one. Give me your address and I'll pick you up at eleven so we can get lunch first."

It wasn't a question, more like an expectation that I would join him for lunch. It should have bothered me that Micah assumed I would go along, right? What kind of man would want someone else to take control like that? So, yeah, I knew it should bother me and that it shouldn't make my dick get hard. Want to guess which one of those was my actual reaction?

"Why don't I pick you up, instead? You said you live close to the office, so you probably aren't too far from the stadium," I said. "No reason for you to drive all the way up to EC North and then turn right around to go back into town."

He agreed and gave me his address, and then we chatted for another couple of minutes. Just small talk, but it was nice. I enjoyed talking with Micah.

After we finally hung up, I had just enough time to throw in a load of laundry and take a long shower. Long because I wanted to take my time relieving my erection. Honestly, if you didn't guess that was my reaction to Micah's somewhat domineering personality, then you haven't been reading carefully. Lost cause over here, remember?

Okay, so before I'd had dinner with Micah Trains on Friday night, if you'd asked me to guess, I would've said he was one of those profile lawyers. You know the type. It's like they came off the lawyer conveyor belt and they have nothing else in their lives except their law practices. And maybe their two divorces.

Anyway, that was before I spent any time with Micah. Now that I knew him a little, I realized there was a lot more to him, and I was really looking forward to spending more time with my new friend. Yes, *friend*. I would keep thinking of Micah in those types of terms—friend, colleague. But not anything more personal and definitely not anything more intimate.

I pulled up to Micah's house and gasped. It was incredible. Seriously, like something out of *Architectural Digest*. The whole thing looked like it was made of concrete cut into angular slabs. Most were gray, but there was a red rectangle jutting out in the front and a green triangle coming from just under the roofline at an angle. I walked up to the door and noticed the plants arranged in perfectly symmetrical rows. Before I had a chance to ring the doorbell, the door opened and Micah Trains was smiling at me.

"Mister Forman. So nice to see you."

I scrunched my nose. "Mister? You're older than me, you know."

Micah laughed and threw his arm around my shoulder. "I don't think it's very polite to call your date old,

Ben, but I'm willing to let it go."

I chuckled nervously, realizing I would have to be very careful. It was just so easy for me to misread any conversation with Micah. My brain's capability to turn every phrase into something unintended seemed limitless.

We walked to my car and got in. As soon as I turned the key in the ignition, music blared from the stereo. I blushed and reached for the dial, turning it down. "Sorry. I like to sing along to the stereo when I drive, and I'm pretty bad, so I crank it up high enough to drown myself out," I explained.

He chuckled and his smile reached his eyes, the little crow's feet on the sides showing. My heart skipped a beat. "Moody Blues fan, huh? Nice. Looks like we won't have to fight over control of the radio. That's critical."

"Just as long as you don't try to make me listen to Celine Dion, we should be safe," I responded.

Micah shuddered. "Then we're all good. As far as I'm concerned, the best way to secure national secrets would be to hide them inside a Celine Dion compilation and put them on the front curb with a sign that says 'Free—take me'."

I cracked up and glanced over at him. "You're a fun man to be around, Micah Trains."

The look in his eyes softened, and my heart skipped another beat. At the rate I was going, I saw a pacemaker in my future.

"You are too, Ben Forman."

CHAPTER FIVE

I HAD never thought of food as something erotic. Don't get me wrong, I like to eat as much as the next guy. But a meal had always been primarily about filling my belly with a secondary benefit of satisfying my taste buds. That lunch with Micah Trains forever changed my perception of food.

When we'd had Indian food for dinner the other night, we'd shared a couple of dishes, eating them family style. Lunch was different. Micah had a club sandwich with fruit salad. I had a burger with fries and a side of constant hard-on. Seriously, constant hard-on.

It started with the fruit. Micah popped a strawberry into his mouth and moaned. My dick woke up and started paying attention.

"These are delicious. Perfectly ripe. And I think they're organic."

Did he say orgasmic? I licked my lips.

"You want to taste one?"

I think I nodded. Hard to remember, really, because I was concentrating on swallowing. Did Micah make moans like that in bed too? Oh, God.

"Here you go," he said, holding a strawberry up. I

expected him to drop it on my plate, but he didn't. Instead, he smudged it against my lips like it was Chapstick. Or his dick. Yeah, my mind was in total overdrive. "Open up." I swear, his voice was huskier.

Why I didn't just laugh it off and swipe the strawberry from him, I couldn't say. Micah told me to open my mouth, so I opened my mouth. He made a final round with the strawberry over my lips. Then he put it on my tongue and waited until I closed my mouth to pull his fingers out slowly. I almost came in my pants.

Micah was quiet for a bit after that. He just sat and stared at me chewing the strawberry. I did my damnedest not to choke under that intense scrutiny.

Then choking became secondary to breathing in my list of priorities, because Micah reached over, picked up a few fries from my plate, and started eating them. Now, you tell me, who eats french fries by dipping them in ketchup, then fellating them to suck it off before actually chewing on the fry? Nobody, right? But that's exactly what Micah did.

Was he intentionally stirring me up? It couldn't all be my imagination, could it? Maybe he was trying to be funny, or maybe he was making fun of me, or maybe he was... I tried to stop my mind from thinking it, but then he sucked off another fry and I couldn't hold back a groan or the thought that Micah Trains was flirting with me.

"You aren't eating your lunch." His voice was calm and even, but his eyes were sizzling.

"Oh, umm, I…" And that eloquent stammer was why Micah was a litigator and my career choice didn't involve impressing a jury.

"You want me to keep feeding you, Ben?"

Oh, God, yes. Yes, please.

But I didn't say those words. We were sitting in the middle of a restaurant. And I wasn't gay. Okay, fine, the last one was crap. And continuing to deny it, at least to myself, was well past ridiculous at that point. But seriously, we were in the middle of a fairly busy restaurant in broad daylight. I picked up my burger and forced myself to take a bite.

When I set it down and started chewing, Micah reached his hand out, wiped some ketchup from the side of my mouth with his long finger, then sucked that same finger into his own mouth, twirling his tongue around it and keeping his eyes locked with mine. Christ! He was definitely flirting with me.

Have you ever found yourself wondering if your existence is God's way of telling a joke? I mean, seriously, *Micah Trains* was coming on to me, and I wasn't sure if it was the best or the worst thing that had ever happened in my life.

On the one hand, an incredibly sexy, super-smart man whose company I enjoyed and whose body I lusted after seemed to want me. On the other hand, if I gave in to Micah's advances, it would be impossible for me to ever go back to living my life as I had been. Huh. When I thought it about like that, both of those things seemed like positives.

WE HAD to go through the now familiar security check when we got to the stadium. It wasn't a big deal, really, just a single file line and a guy running a wand a couple of inches from our bodies. The problem was that my dick was still hard from the whole thing at lunch and I was nervous that the security guard would notice. Micah must have sensed my discomfort, because as soon as we got through the line and into the stadium, he started joking around.

"I had to go take some depos in Canada last year, and let me tell you, getting back into the country is way more invasive than this security process. The US Border Patrol skips the whole foreplay-masquerading-as-frisking bit and goes with a detailed question and answer session instead. I actually found that to be a hell of a lot more intimate. I mean, having a guy grab my dick on the first date is one thing, but asking all sorts of fucking details about how I spend my time is off the table until we're at the whole toothbrush-at-each-other's-places stage, you know? With as thorough as those guys were, you'd think I was trying to smuggle marriage equality, responsible gun laws, and universal health care into the country."

I was smiling and chuckling, all my discomfort over the security check forgotten. It was amazing how that man could make me laugh and alleviate my anxieties so easily. And it was also amazing that he was gay. If there had been any remaining doubt about that, which there essentially wasn't after that sex show he put on at lunch, it was gone after he made that last comment. I wondered whether this information was common knowledge. Probably not, or I surely would have heard about it at some point over the years when my colleagues had gossiped about the hotshot litigator or, at the very least, while we were interviewing him to join our firm.

We got a couple of beers and a bag of peanuts to share and headed to our seats. I won't lie to you. When I saw where we were sitting, I almost bounced up and down like a little girl. All right, maybe there was a bit of *actual* bouncing involved. But it was subtle.

I'm a sports guy. I like playing them. I like watching them. I like talking about them. And I enjoy all types of sports. But the thing I've always enjoyed most is watching Major League Baseball games. And we were sitting close enough to smell the grass and hear the conversations from the field. It was incredible.

"These seats are unbelievable, Micah." My face hurt from how broadly I was smiling. "I'd imagine only people who bought in when the stadium first opened can own these. How'd you get the tickets?"

For a second it looked like Micah was blushing, but I wrote it off as being heat-related. The man was way too self-assured and confident to ever be embarrassed about anything. "I helped out one of the team VPs with a legal matter last year, and he owed me a favor, so I called it in." He licked his lips and looked right into my eyes. "You were saying how much you like the Glory on Friday and that you planned to watch this game, so I figured you'd want to go."

My jaw dropped. He had sought out these almost-impossible-to-get tickets just for me?

Micah reached his hand over and stroked my chin as he gently pushed it up to help close my mouth. "Don't look so surprised. I like spending time with you, Ben. I'm happy to procure whatever tickets I need to make that happen." After a few heartbeats, he relaxed into his chair, stretched his long legs in front of him, and tossed a peanut into his mouth. "All right, so tell me the odds you're giving our boys out there today. Think we can kick some ass, or are we gonna take another pummeling?"

I pried my eyes away from that sexy-as-hell body and looked at the field. "What kind of question is that?" I said. "Have you no loyalty? Of course we're gonna beat 'em."

I HAD never had more fun at a baseball game. Micah seemed interested in my embarrassingly detailed knowledge of every player's stats. I loved his creativity when he yelled at the umpires over questionable calls. Our fingers touched constantly when we reached for the peanuts. And the Glory won with a home run in the bottom of the ninth. It was a great afternoon.

It was only four o'clock when the game ended, which was still early. I didn't want my day with Micah to end yet. As we wound through the streets and chit-chatted about the game, I kept trying to come up with something to say that would keep me from having to drop him at his house and say goodbye.

"Do you like to swim?" he asked during a break in the conversation.

"Yeah, sure. I'm not great at it, but I like getting in the water."

"Me too. I have a pool, put it in last year. You wanna go for a dip?"

My head jerked to the side so I could look at him, and then I turned back to the road. "Right now?"

"Sure. Why not? Pool's heated. We can swim and hang out and then order a pizza or something for dinner. What do you say?"

There were a million reasons to say no. Seeing Micah with less clothing was bound to ramp up my already out of control libido. If I was wearing a swimsuit, said out of control libido would be noticeably ramped. I didn't have a swimsuit with me. "That sounds great. I haven't been in a pool since last summer."

I know, I know. I just said there were a million reasons to say no. But there was also a reason to say yes—getting to spend more time with Micah. As it turned out, that reason took the gold in my mental Olympics.

We walked into the house, and Micah gave me a quick tour, which ended in his sleek kitchen.

"Your place is great. It's really unique."

"Thanks. I was annoyingly picky when I was house hunting, much to my Realtor's chagrin. Then one day he brought me to this lot. We pulled up and I saw a dilapidated piece of crap. One side of the house was practically falling down, the windows were cracked, it was a complete fuckin' disaster. Turns out David, my Realtor, figured the only way I'd be happy would be to build my own house, so he found me a tear-down. The rest, as they say, is history."

I nodded and smiled, acting calm on the outside. But inside was another story entirely. My heart raced, and my stomach felt like it was tied in knots. I wasn't sure whether my feelings were the result of standing so close to a man I found incredibly intriguing and painfully attractive or whether they were due to the realization that I might actually do something about those feelings.

What would it be like, I wondered, to stop holding back, to feel something and act on it? Just like that. What would happen if I let myself go?

Would everyone find out about my feelings toward men? Would clients stop wanting to work with me? Would my friends make excuses to stop seeing me? Would I break my parents' hearts?

"Here you go, Ben."

I blinked and refocused on the present. Micah was

standing inches away from me and holding a water bottle out. I licked my lips and realized that my mouth was dry. How did he know?

"Thanks," I croaked out and curled my fingers around the cool plastic.

Micah released the bottle, but he didn't move back. He was standing so close to me, closer than he had been the other night in the parking garage. And his blue eyes looked darker than usual. I wanted so much to reach my hand out and caress the hair on his cheek. Would his beard feel soft, or would it be rough?

He focused his eyes on my mouth, then raised them to meet my gaze. He started leaning toward me, and my lips parted of their own initiative. My heart slammed against my chest. My dick made a valiant effort to break out of my zipper. And then I took a step back, raised the water bottle to my mouth, and gulped down a couple sips.

I tried to ignore the confusion mapped across Micah's face. I simply wasn't up to explaining something to him that I didn't understand myself. I wanted his kiss more than anything, so why did I prevent it from happening?

I was a mess. Why would a man as successful, handsome, and fun as Micah Trains want to spend any time with me? I could barely stand being with myself.

Be honest, you wish you could give me a smack right now, don't you? I wouldn't blame you. Hell, maybe it would help. Nothing else seemed to work.

CHAPTER SIX

MICAH SNATCHED the phone from the counter. "How hungry are you? I'll call in the pizza order now, but we can ask them to deliver later if you're still full from lunch plus all those snacks you inhaled at the game."

"Hey!" I cried out in mock outrage. "We shared those snacks."

"Uh huh. If you define *shared* as me eating one chip and you devouring the rest of the nachos like the processed cheese was a French delicacy. Ditto on the popcorn."

"Whatever, you ate at least half of the peanuts." I got closer to him and lightly smacked his chest. He covered my hand with his and kept it steady against him. I could feel his heart beating and the warmth of his skin seeping through his shirt. I swallowed hard but didn't let myself step any closer. "I'll be ready for dinner in a couple of hours. That work for you?"

He nodded, removed his hand from mine, and used it to hit a preset number button on his phone. I guessed that pizza delivery was a regular meal for him. Made sense—Micah probably had no time to cook with the hours he worked. My billables were way lower than his, and my stove was on the cusp of filing a neglect complaint due to lack of use.

"Yeah. Delivery, please. An extra-large deep-dish with mushrooms, a Greek salad, garlic toast, and a couple of orders of tiramisu." Micah covered the phone with his hand and looked at me with a smirk. "What'll you have?"

I chuckled. "Ha ha, funny man. That order sounds good."

He confirmed his address, read off his credit card number, and hung up the phone. "All right, we've got two hours. You still up for a dip in the pool?"

I nodded. "Absolutely. But I don't have a suit with me."

Micah's hand shot out and clasped my hip, pulling me closer to him. "Why, Benjamin Forman, are you suggesting we skinny dip?" He sounded scandalized even though I knew he was anything but.

My dick definitely liked the idea of being naked with Micah. But the rest of me was nervous. I could feel the heat rising on my neck, and I hoped the blush wouldn't be noticeable. "I, uh, I..."

Damn it! Why couldn't I string together a simple sentence?

Micah kept his expression calm and even. He tapped my hip and then walked out of the kitchen, talking to me over his shoulder. "We're about the same size. I'm sure one of my swimsuits will fit you."

He was back in a few minutes, wearing nothing but a square-cut swimsuit and holding another suit out to me. The man had a seriously fine body. It wasn't quite as broad as mine, but it was more cut, with wiry muscles and a flat stomach. There was a smattering of brown hair on his chest, and it narrowed down to a trail leading into his waistband. My eyes took a trip down that path and settled on the bulge in his suit.

I wanted to touch him, wanted the heat of his skin to warm my fingers. Would his erection feel different from my own? What would it be like to hold it in my hand, to take it into my mouth, to feel it inside my body?

I squeezed my eyes shut and cleared my throat. "I'll change and meet you out there in a sec. Thanks for the suit," I said, wondering if my voice sounded as gravelly to him as it did to my ears.

I snagged the swimsuit from Micah and walked into the bathroom, hoping he hadn't noticed that I was trembling. With the suit still tangled between my fingers, I white-knuckled the counter, dipped my head, and concentrated on slowing my breathing. I could think about what was going on with me and freak out later tonight, but not now, not in front of Micah Trains. Right now I had to force my overactive mind to take a sabbatical so I could bask in the company of a man I truly enjoyed.

Micah was swimming laps when I got out to the pool. I stood on the cool deck and watched him cut through the water gracefully, reach the far end of the pool, then flip underwater and do it all again. After a few minutes, he stopped, wiped the water from his face, and blinked up at me.

"Come on in. The pool's heated, so the water's great."

I jumped in the pool and immediately regretted it. If I had the power to fly, I would have been airborne in seconds. But as it was, I used my all-too-human skills and lurched toward the side of the pool, gripped the deck with one hand, and propelled my legs to the side and up.

"You jerk! The water's freezing." I was sputtering and shivering, sitting on the deck and rubbing my hands over my arms. I was so busy concentrating on warming up that I didn't stop to think about how ridiculous I probably looked.

That was, until Micah started laughing hysterically. "It's over seventy degrees. That's nowhere near freezing, you pansy ass. Grow a pair and get back in here."

I couldn't hold back a grin. The same man who'd been coming on to me all day, who'd gone out of his way to plan a date he knew I would enjoy, was teasing me like a buddy in the locker room. It was so different from my other dating experiences—more fun, more interesting, and, in a strange twist, more comfortable.

"I might actually need to grow a new pair if I get back into that pool, because my balls are gonna take refuge inside my chest cavity."

"Oh, come on. It's not that bad. Give it a shot," he

said with complete conviction, as if the power of his words alone could make me forget that I had almost turned into a Popsicle. The crazy thing was that he was almost effective. The man must have been a sight to behold in a courtroom.

"I did give it a shot, and now I need to check my appendages for frostbite. No way am I going in there again. Once was quite enough, thank you."

"You know what they say, Ben, it only hurts the first time," he said with a lecherous grin. "Now quit sniveling and get in here. I'll find a way to keep you warm if you're really worried about it."

I decided to get in the water. Not because I had suddenly developed memory loss and forgotten that it was freeze-my-nuts-off cold in there, but more because I wanted to dunk Micah underneath and wipe that smirk off his face.

Five minutes later, I was gasping for air and Micah was calling for a draw from our underwater wrestling match. His arm was wrapped around my chest. Mine was clutching his neck. Our legs were all tangled, and our bodies were pressed together.

"I'll let go if you admit defeat, loudmouth." I think being as breathless as I was decreased the intimidating tone I had been hoping to achieve.

"I think you have that backward, Forman. I was willing to call it a tie in order to spare your fragile ego, but if you're going to be a dickhead about it, the offer's off the table."

I twisted around and elbowed his ribs. He huffed and

then somehow took my legs out from under me. Then we were both underwater, our hands locked together, each of us trying to get in a jab while simultaneously trying to defend against the other. Eventually, one or both of us needed to breathe, and I found myself with my upper body draped on the deck, gasping for air. It was satisfying to see Micah was in the same condition.

"I won." I managed to get the words out despite the need to draw oxygen into my lungs.

"Fuck you." It was an efficient reply, and it contained neither a concession nor a gloat.

"You do have excellent mastery of the English language, Micah. I'll give you that."

"I have an excellent mastery of other things too," he said with an attempt at a leer. It was hard to pull off when he still looked like a noodle collapsed on the deck. "Give me a chance and I'll show you."

Damn, but he had beautiful eyes. Like a blue ocean with glistening waves.

"I haven't ever done this."

My voice was low, but my heart was speeding. I had surprised myself with that confession. It wasn't planned, wasn't thought out, it just sort of sprang from my mouth in an inopportune moment of honesty.

I flinched in expectation of his response. Would he laugh at me for essentially being a virgin at thirty-one? Of course I wasn't actually a virgin. I had slept with women.

But it wasn't the same thing. Or maybe he would be like my brother—disgusted by the fact that I had hidden myself for so long.

I didn't have too much time to stress about it, because Micah moved and put his hands on my hips. He gazed into my eyes.

"I've never dated anyone from work either. I know it could get awkward, but we're both partners at the firm, so it's not like there's any issue with inappropriate use of authority." He rested his forehead on mine. "I really like you, Ben. And I think you like me. Can we see where this thing between us can go?"

I didn't correct his misimpression of what I had never done. I didn't tell him that awkwardness at work was only one of my issues, but the bigger one was being with any man. I didn't even say that he was right about my feelings for him. In fact, I didn't say anything at all.

My body just took over, and I found myself nodding. Then Micah's hands stroked up my arms, across my neck, and landed on the sides of my face. He caressed my cheeks, gave me a look that made my stomach flip over, and then he leaned in and kissed me.

It was a soft kiss, no tongue. Just his lips brushing against mine with a gentle pressure, backing off, and then doing it again. His beard on my face and his hard, muscular body pressed against mine stole my breath and tightened my chest.

There was no way for me to pretend I was kissing a woman. Everything about Micah was unequivocally male. And it seemed that even if my brain hadn't completely made up its mind about the situation, my body had, because it was the first time in my memory that I got rock hard while making out with somebody from nothing more than a kiss.

We stayed in the pool, our lower bodies underwater and our upper bodies pressed together. Our lips kept meeting in tender kisses; Micah's hands continued petting my face, my neck, my arms, and my back. And somewhere along the way, I forgot to feel cold or anxious or anything other than content.

I let myself explore Micah's skin, let my fingers comb through the hair on his chest and stroke his beard, let my tongue dart out occasionally and taste his lips. Micah took my lower lip between both of his and tugged gently. Then he let go and kissed his way across my jaw and over to my ear. His tongue licked my lobe, and then he sucked it gently into his mouth.

"You feel so damn good, Ben," he murmured.

"So do you," I said with a raspy voice.

It was true. He felt amazing. Our bodies seemed to fit together just right, our heads at the perfect height for kissing, our hips lined up together, his leg pushed between both of mine, putting a wonderful pressure on my cock. It was perfect.

I leaned in and kissed him again, not wanting the

intimate moment to stop. Micah seemed to be of the same mind, because he groaned, curled his hands around the back of my head, and held me still as he increased the intensity of the kisses. It wasn't long before our tongues tangled, our breathing got heavier, and our hips moved together in an incredibly erotic dance.

By the time I realized what was about to happen, it was too late. There was no way for me to stop the runaway orgasm train racing through my body. Micah must have realized it too, because he increased the pressure his thigh was putting on my dick, and put one hand on my ass and the other on the back of my neck, encouraging my thrusting motions. I buried my face in his neck and whimpered as my movements got faster, more desperate.

"Come on. Come on," he whispered into my ear and kissed my temple.

It was the tender kiss that pushed me over the edge, and I came with a joyous shout. Then my entire body went limp against Micah. He held me and rubbed circles on my back as I trembled and tried to get air back into my lungs.

I had never experienced an orgasm like that. Never. The fact that it had happened from rubbing off on somebody while I was still dressed made that fact all the more startling.

"I...I'm sorry." My words were mumbled because my face was still pressed against Micah's skin.

"Sorry? Why? That was hot as hell." He removed his hand from its perch on my ass and pushed it between our stomachs and into his suit. "You're so fuckin' gorgeous, Ben."

He dipped his head so his mouth was right against my neck, his breath hot on my skin. I could feel his hand moving between us as he stroked himself, and I knew that I had to join in.

With my hands shaking, I tucked my thumbs into the waistband of his suit and pulled it out and down, letting his dick spring free. Then I took a deep breath and wrapped my fingers around his glans. Oh God. I was holding his dick in my hand.

He thrust up and back a few times, pushing himself through both of our fists, and then he shuddered and called my name as warmth covered my fingers.

Neither of us moved after that. We just stood together, each of our heads leaning on the other's shoulder, both of us breathing hard, and Micah occasionally dropping a kiss on my neck.

It was the most wonderful moment of my life. And it terrified me.

CHAPTER SEVEN

THE REST of the evening with Micah was very low-key. We sat out on his patio, ate pizza, and talked about nothing and everything. Then he walked me to the door, we shared a quick kiss, and I got into my car to make the drive back to EC North. I left the radio off as I headed toward my condo. There was enough noise inside my head without me adding to the chaos by layering music on top of it.

I had always had trouble sleeping, so even though the busy day had left me feeling exhausted, I still lay in bed for hours, unable to shut off my mind. Eventually, I drifted into a restless slumber, which was par for the course as far as my sleep pattern went. Given the too little amount of rest, I should have been grumpy in the morning. But I wasn't.

I woke up with Micah's smile in my mind. It wasn't his public smile, the one he shared with colleagues or clients. No, it was that soft, tender smile that made his eyes crinkle and my heart ache. In that moment, I knew I would stick to my agreement to see where things could go with Micah. I simply didn't have the strength to walk away from the opportunity to see him smile at me that way again.

My morning routine went by on autopilot. Shower,

shave, clothes, two bowls of cereal, and I was at the door with my keys in my hand. There was a full-length mirror hanging by my front door, something my mother had bought when I moved in under the theory that it would create an optional illusion of additional space. I walked past that mirror at least twice a day, coming and going from my condo. But that morning I stopped instead of walking by, and I took a careful look at myself.

Thick, chestnut-brown hair, finger length on top, slightly shorter on the sides and back, styled in a fairly typical, traditional cut. Brown eyes, a straight nose, full lips, and a prominent jawline. And that topped off broad shoulders, a muscular chest, narrow waist, and strong legs.

People had told me I was handsome my entire life, and I didn't disagree. I had enough problems to put a therapist's kid through college, but body dysmorphia wasn't one of them. I looked good on the outside. It was the clusterfuck going on inside my head that was on its way to giving me an ulcer.

I knew that I needed to deal with my issues, that I needed to make a decision about how I was going to live my life and stick with it, that I needed to find some way to feel as happy and content as my brother seemed to be. That thought had me closing my eyes and shaking my head.

My parents were wrong about gay people being lonely or depressed or rejected from society. Well, at least they were wrong about my brother, because Noah was none of those things. And his gay friends didn't seem to have those types of problems either. For that matter, neither did Micah Trains. He was confident, well-respected professionally, and I had heard him talk about various friends in passing during the time I had spent with him.

I wanted to know how they did it. How they managed to avoid the curse that I had always believed to be part and parcel of the gay lifestyle. Hell, I had never admitted to anyone that I was gay, let alone acted on it, and the curse seemed to be alive and kicking within me.

The obvious way to get an answer to my question was to ask my brother. But I didn't have the energy to get ridiculed by Noah once again, and there was no doubt in my mind that that would be the inevitable consequence of going to him for advice. And I couldn't ask Micah, because that question would highlight for him exactly how clueless, inexperienced, and messed up I was. No, I would have to figure it out on my own.

THE GOOD thing about being swamped at work was that it didn't leave any room for me to focus on my personal issues. Even though I was drowning in contract negotiations and deal closings, my brain felt like it was finally able to rest. Pretty pathetic, isn't it? Believe me, you aren't thinking anything different from what I had already realized about myself. I just didn't know how to fix it. Then, around midmorning, I succeeded in making things worse.

Call the Guinness people, because surely I must qualify for some sort of world record. "Person most unable to manage his own life" perhaps. Or maybe "guy least likely to find his own ass with a map and a flashlight."

"Good morning." I heard Micah's raspy voice along with a knock on my slightly open door. "How do you feel about going on a Starbucks run?"

I looked up to see his brilliant smile aimed at me. He was wearing a gray suit, a sky-blue shirt, and a light and dark gray hound's-tooth tie. If ever there was a man made to wear a suit, it was Micah Trains. He looked incredible—powerful, handsome, brilliant, and intimidating, all mingled together in a sexy-as-hell package. I wanted to get up from my chair, fall at his feet, and worship him by rubbing my face against that bulge in his pants. A mental image of me doing just that came unbidden into my mind, causing my body to become excited and my brain to become horrified.

"Hi." I managed to push the word out of my mouth.

Micah walked into my office and hovered next to my desk. I wasn't sure what he wanted until he finally let out a sigh, planted both hands on the top of my desk, and leaned in toward me. He was going to kiss me. Right there at the office in front of everyone. Yeah, okay, we were the only two people in my office, the door was barely cracked open, and the people on either side of me were out. But still.

I jerked my head away and darted my eyes toward my office door in a panic. When I was sure that nobody had seen Micah's little display, I looked back at him. The pain on his face was clear, but I didn't feel like there was anything I could do about it. Kissing him when we were alone at his house was one thing—there was no chance of anybody finding out. But doing it anywhere else was just asking for trouble.

After a few seconds, he sank into one of the chairs across from my desk and rubbed his palm over the back of his neck. It seemed like he was waiting for me to say something. But when I didn't, he sucked in some air, let it out, and then leaned forward, clasping his hands together and resting his forearms on his knees.

"Look, Ben, I know you're worried about dating someone from the firm, but we've already talked about this. There's no policy against it, we're both partners, we're in different practice groups, so our work doesn't overlap at all. I just don't think it's going to be an issue. Besides, people are going to figure out we're in a relationship eventually, so we may as well just be up-front about it from the beginning."

Okay, so how would you respond to that little speech? Would you maybe apologize for having overreacted? Or maybe you'd go with the honest approach and explain that it wasn't just the people from work at issue and you were having trouble with the idea that anyone, including yourself, thought of you as gay? Or maybe you'd try to brush the uncomfortable moment under the rug with a joke and then get up and go for that coffee run so the awkwardness could be forgotten?

Yeah, well, any one of those options would have been superior to my choice of action. To be fair, though, I was going for that Guinness World Record in "biggest dumbass on the planet," and I'm fairly sure my next move managed to lock it up. "Who said anything about a relationship? We just...hung out a little. It was nothing," I said.

Nothing. Everything. Sure, anybody could get confused about the difference between those two things. After all, they're practically identical. And by practically, I mean not at all.

I couldn't bring myself to look Micah in the face when I was talking, and then it was too late, because he got up and slowly walked out of my office. He paused by the door with his back to me. "I'm sorry for my mistake. I'll see you around, Ben."

And then he was gone.

I waited to feel relief at the fact that I no longer had to figure out how to deal with Micah. I waited for my feelings to go away or get shoved so deep into my stomach that I didn't have to think about them except during those times when things got really bad and I coughed up blood. I waited for my body and my mind to shake this off, just like I had shaken off so many things and then gone back to acting like the man I was supposed to be.

But none of that happened. I still hated the man I was. I still wanted Micah Trains and didn't know how to stop myself. And I still wasn't sure that I wanted to be stopped.

I folded my arms on my desk and dropped my head on top of them, blocking out the light and trying to get myself together. When I heard a thumping noise and realized it was my head hitting the desk over and over again, I knew I had made the wrong call in dealing with Micah. Hey, if what's obviously in front of you fails to get your attention, try a self-inflicted traumatic brain injury. It's a time-tested approach sure to solve even the most difficult dilemmas.

NEITHER GIVING myself a concussion nor burying myself in my work all day made a dent in my feelings. When I found myself reading the same sentence for the fourth time and still not having any idea what it said, I knew it was time to pack it in for the day. I shut down my computer and looked at my watch. Six thirty. It was late enough for the staff to have gone home and probably most of the attorneys too, but my guess was that Micah "Workaholic" Trains was still in his office plugging away.

I was walking toward his office before I had come up with any sort of strategy. Earlier that morning, he had come into my office with a sweet smile and a Starbucks invitation and I had acted like a complete asshole. All right, so just marching up to him and saying, "Whatcha doin'?" probably wouldn't be the best approach for me to take. In light of that, I turned toward the elevator bank instead.

Fifteen minutes later, I was standing in front of Micah's office door, shifting from foot to foot nervously and looking at the back of his head as he typed away at his computer.

"You planning on just standing there enjoying the view all day, or is there something I can do for you, Mister Forman?" His gravelly voice had a distinct gruffness to it.

I walked in and sat down in the chair across from his desk, but he still didn't turn around. Well, I supposed it was time to eat crow. Fair enough. "I thought you might want that coffee you mentioned earlier, so I picked some up. I wasn't sure what you wanted, so I brought options. I have an Americano, a mocha, a latte, a macchiato—"

He swiveled his chair so he was finally facing me and interrupted my menu list. "I'm not a coffee drinker. I like tea."

His voice sounded angry, but I felt like there was a hint of tenderness in his eyes. That gave me enough hope to keep trying. I reached into one of the four-pack drink carriers I had brought with me and held two cups up to him.

"Black or chai?"

That earned me a chuckle and a smile. He took one of the cups from me and sipped at it. "So this is an apology for earlier?" he asked quietly.

"Uh huh." I nodded. "I was a jerk and I don't know

what to say and..."

He nodded. "It's okay. I understand. Believe me, I've had my share of pissy days. Apology accepted."

There was a part of me that wished he hadn't been so understanding, because it made me feel like even more of an ass. Being cruel was never okay, even if I had been having a bad day, which I hadn't. My day had been typical. The reason I had lashed out at Micah had nothing to do with my day and everything to do with my reluctance to admit my feelings for him.

I wanted so much to ask his advice. Maybe there had been a time when he had been scared too. Maybe he would understand what I was going through. But when I looked at Micah sitting in his corner office, jacket hanging on the back of his chair, sleeves rolled up to his elbows, tie loosened, top two shirt buttons open, I saw only confidence and strength. It was impossible to imagine such a smart, successful guy feeling scared of anything.

So I didn't utter another word about that morning. Instead, I sipped at the tea Micah hadn't taken and relaxed back in the chair. "Are you going to break for dinner, or do you need to work through?" I asked.

Micah arched one eyebrow. "Well, that depends. Are you inviting me to dinner?"

That had certainly been my hope. But hearing him say it still made me blush. I had essentially just asked another man out on a date. Embarrassment aside, I had to answer the question. And since I wanted to spend more time with Micah, dinner seemed like a perfect plan. "Yes, I'm inviting you to dinner. What do you say?"

He grinned and got up from his desk, snagged his jacket, and threw it over one shoulder. "You're on. And I'll just warn you right now that I plan on being a very expensive date. I skipped lunch today and I'm so fuckin' hungry that I'll probably end up eating almost as much as you on an average day." He winked at me with the last part.

I laughed and stood up. "All right, smart guy. Let's go. Your supersize meal is waiting."

CHAPTER EIGHT

MICAH WALKED over to me, gripped my waist, and pulled me flush against him. My heart rate immediately skyrocketed, and I held my breath. I knew what was coming, but unlike that morning, I didn't let myself pull away.

There was still a part of me that was very aware of the fact that I was at work in the arms of another man. But it was late; almost everyone was probably gone for the day. And besides, Micah smelled so damn good.

When his lips met mine and I felt his tongue slip out and lick my bottom lip, I moaned and opened to him. My hands left my sides and landed on his chest, my head tilted so he could plunder my mouth even deeper, and my hips joined his in a slow circular dance.

When we finally broke apart, I whimpered. He raised his hand from my waist to my face, cupped my cheek, and stroked my lips with his thumb. The look in his eyes was nothing short of smoldering. "Damn, Ben, you are a fuckin' fantastic kisser."

With him, maybe. I really hadn't been one for kissing before. A hello peck, yeah, but not a full-on, tongue-swapping, breath-stealing kiss. I leaned forward to eliminate the new space between our faces, taking another kiss and then another until our mouths were locked together again.

When our hips joined the party, rubbing our groins together, I knew it was time to stop. But I couldn't. I just whimpered, clutched his shirt, and kissed him harder.

Eventually, I felt both of his strong hands on my waist, holding me still. He pulled his mouth away and kissed across my jaw. "We need to stop. I'm about one more grind away from bending you over my desk, and even I think that's probably taking things too far at work." He kissed my neck and then gave me a little bite. "Well, at least on a Monday evening. If you want to get kinky that way, we can try it on the weekend or much later at night, when the place is deserted."

My groin tightened further and I knew my dick liked that idea. "Oh, God. I have to be so careful with you, Micah, or else I'm going to be in huge trouble."

I hadn't realized I had spoken my thoughts out loud until he raised his face so he could look at mine and answered me. "If anyone's in trouble here, I'm pretty sure it's me. I can see myself seriously falling for you." The intensity of his gaze deepened. "Question is, are you interested in being there to catch me?"

A ringing sound interrupted the sober moment. Micah sighed and squatted down on the floor, where he had apparently dropped his jacket at some point during our groping session. He looked up at me apologetically as he dug his phone out of his jacket pocket and stood back up.

"I'm sorry, but I need to get this. It's my mom's ringtone, and it's the third time she's tried to reach me today."

"Go ahead." I nodded toward the phone. "Do you need me to leave?"

He put his hand on the small of my back and shook his head as he pressed a button on his phone and held it up to his ear.

"Hi, Mom." Pause. "I'm sorry I couldn't call you back earlier. I had a filing I had to get out by five." Pause. "I'm not working too hard." Pause. "I mean it, I'm fine." Pause. "Yeah, I am, but I'm leaving now." Pause. "I'm going to get some dinner." Pause. "Because my cooking can't measure up to yours, so I don't bother trying." A smirk and a pause, then a laugh. "Silver tongue or not, I mean it. Listen, Mom, I need to go, but I'll call you later." Pause. "I love you too. Bye."

I put both hands around his neck and looked into a gorgeous set of twinkling blue eyes. "Silver tongue? So that's the secret weapon you've been using to turn my knees into rubber every time we kiss."

Micah dropped the phone into his pants pocket and moved his hand to my crotch, outlining my still visible erection with a fingertip and then cupping it and giving it a squeeze. "Hopefully, I'm impacting a body part located higher than your knees." My body trembled in reaction to his touch. Then he leaned down to pick up his jacket and smirked up at me. "And if you like feeling like you're having trouble walking, then you'll be ecstatic when I properly introduce you to my *real* secret weapon."

I snorted out a laugh. "Wow, you sure are a smooth talker. You get a lot of success with lines like that?"

We started walking toward the door, and Micah wrapped his arm around my waist and held me close. "I don't know yet. I'll get back to you on that tomorrow morning."

He waggled his eyebrows in an exaggerated Groucho Marx impression, and I found myself laughing all the way to the elevator bank. It wasn't until the elevator doors closed, taking us out of our office, that I realized we had walked down the empty hallway pressed together with Micah's arm draped possessively around me and I hadn't been uncomfortable. In fact, I had felt secure and warm.

I wondered if that safe, happy feeling blossoming in my chest was how my brother felt when he was with Clark. Those two always seemed to be touching each other, and for the first time, I realized that they might behave that way in public because of their feelings for one another rather than as some sort of political statement. Even though nobody had seen me and Micah walking out together, I felt like I had just experienced a growth moment. And not just in my pants.

WITH WORK, it was too hard for either of us to stay over at each other's places in the middle of the week. At least, that was the excuse I used when I said I couldn't come over to Micah's house after dinner. Truth was I was buying time because I was nervous about taking what I knew would be the next step with him.

But that didn't stop me from spending time with Micah. We had dinner together again every night that week. Then he went out of town on Friday, or we would probably have broken bread on the weekend too.

Keeping my hands—and other body parts—off Micah had grown progressively harder (no pun intended) the more time I spent with him. We'd had a few more heavy kissing sessions in the office and in the parking garage after our dinners out, but it hadn't gone any further.

So I had gotten in my car every night and made the ridiculously long drive home sporting a hard-on that could cut glass. When I got home alone and finally took myself in hand, I still couldn't reach a satisfactory release. It seemed that beating off, which had to that point in my life been my favorite way to get off, wasn't really doing the job anymore because I wanted Micah's touch rather than my own.

Micah was traveling for a week, taking depos across the country. Without him there, my life felt empty. I went home to my lonely apartment every night, ate a microwave meal standing at the counter, and watched TV until my phone rang.

It was always him, telling me about his day, asking me about mine. Just catching up. I missed him.

By the time Thursday rolled around, I knew that I had to be with Micah, whatever the repercussions. The way I felt when I was with him was too wonderful for me to abandon. I couldn't. He would be home the next night, and based on what he had said during our telephone calls, I knew he would want us to spend the weekend together.

I left the office at five thirty and hit the gym. Throughout my workout and during my drive home afterward, I kept thinking about Micah. Funny little things he'd told me. Stories he'd shared about his childhood. The awe in the managing partner's voice when she'd told some of the other attorneys about how Micah had handled a particularly sticky oral argument. His dick.

Look, I don't pretend to be the most exciting guy around and I was terrified of the changes in my life, but I'm not an automaton. I had touched Micah's naked cock that one time in the pool, and it wasn't enough. I wanted to hold it in my hand again. I wanted to lick it and suck it into my mouth. And I wanted him to do the same to me.

Just thinking about Micah had gotten me hard. Again. I pressed the heel of my hand down on my dick and moaned. All right, masturbating on the highway was dangerous and potentially humiliating, but don't tell me you've never thought of doing it during a long car trip. Anyway, I needed to stop.

I know I just grumbled about my unfulfilled state of arousal, but truthfully, I was grateful for it, because it confirmed that my body was functioning properly. In light of the way I reacted to Micah, I knew I would never have to rely on the bottle of pills I kept hidden in the back of my medicine cabinet in order to have sex with him. No, the only thing I would need for that to happen was to either get over my anxiety or move forward despite it.

I finally made it home and walked up the stairs to my unit on the second floor. My gym bag was in one hand and my condo key in the other when my cell phone rang. I quickly pushed the key into the lock and turned it, shoved the door open with my shoulder, and then dropped everything on the ground and yanked my phone out of my pocket.

"'Lo?"

Micah's husky laugh greeted me. "You sound a little out of breath. Am I interrupting something fun?"

I chuckled. "Not yet. I'm just walking in the door. But I had plans for some fun during my shower."

One of the things I enjoyed about dating Micah—yes, I could admit that we were dating, at least to myself—was our friendship. I could joke around with him like I had with my old teammates and frat brothers. But that joking took on an extra layer of fun, because it often turned into flirting. I hadn't ever had that with any of the women I'd dated, and I found I liked it. I liked so many things about Micah.

"How about we have some fun together instead?" he asked.

I got my mind back onto our conversation and

focused on the meaning of his words. "What do you mean? Like phone sex?"

Micah chuckled again. "Yeah, just like that. So what are you wearing?"

I pressed the phone between my shoulder and my ear and turned back to my still open front door. "Oh, come on."

I kicked the door shut and flipped the lock. Then I bent down and picked up my gym bag and keys. I dropped the keys on the table by the front door and took the gym bag into the bedroom with me.

"That's exactly what I'm trying to do, Ben, but you're not cooperating."

I rolled my eyes. "I'm wearing assless chaps, a leather vest, and a dog collar. What are you wearing?"

I assumed Micah had been taking a drink or something, because he suddenly started coughing and gasping for air. I unpacked my gym bag and waited for him to catch his breath.

"Oh, wow," he finally sputtered. "That was some image you just painted for me."

"Yeah? You into that kind of thing?"

"No, I much prefer buttoned-up pretty-boy types. With brown hair and brown eyes. About six foot, three inches tall. With soft pouty lips. And hard bodies."

I unlaced my shoes and kicked them off. Then I flopped back on my bed and threw one hand over my head and held the phone with the other. "All right, all right, Casanova. I get the picture. So tell me how today's depos went."

Micah sighed. "No phone sex?"

I hated to disappoint him, but I wasn't completely sure how everything would work with in-person sex between two men. Trying to turn him on with nothing more than words sounded like a recipe for failure, which wasn't something I was willing to risk. Making sure that Micah continued to be interested in me had managed to turn into my top priority. Even if I was still scared of being with him.

"No phone sex," I replied.

"Fine. But if we don't have some kind of sex soon, my dick might run away and join the circus just to get some excitement."

I realized that I was smiling again. Happiness seemed to just overtake me whenever I was talking with Micah. It all came so naturally with him—being friends, joking around, being together, touching. Everything. "Nah. He won't like it there. They'll stuff him in a tight space with a bunch of clowns or make him put his head in a tiger's mouth, and those teeth are really pointy."

"Yeah, that would suck," Micah said. "And not in the good way. So, speaking of sucking, what are you doing tomorrow night?"

I shook my head even though he couldn't see me. "Not much for subtlety, are you? I'm free tomorrow. What do you have in mind? And does it involve Popsicles? Or maybe lollipops?"

"I can't tell you what I have in my mind right now,

because you said no phone sex. But I'll give you a hint and say that it involves cocks—as in yours and mine—and not sugary treats."

"Baby, when you taste my dick, I think you'll agree that it's the sweetest treat around," I said in a campy, overly exaggerated seductive tone.

"Oh, that was bad. Really bad." Micah laughed. "We're gonna have to work on your dirty talk this weekend, Mister Forman."

"I'll add it to the schedule. What else do you want to do?" I asked.

"You." His voice had lowered, and he sounded even sexier.

A tremble coursed through my body. "Okay. It's a plan. What time are you getting back into town?"

He sighed. "I have a couple more depos in the morning and there wasn't a direct flight available, so I won't be back in Emile City until close to five. And I need to go to Shabbat services tomorrow, but they should be over by seven thirty. My weekend's wide open after that, so I'm yours for as long as you want me."

That would be forever. I swallowed down that instinctive response and was struck momentarily mute from the shock of how strongly I felt it.

I had never thought of anything in terms of forever. I had always just taken my life as it came, not thinking too much about the future. Hell, it was all I could do to get through the present without disappointing a bunch of people. Thinking about the future would have been way too overwhelming.

But in that moment, I found myself thinking about a future with Micah. I thought about having him around every day to laugh with. I thought about being able to talk through issues and questions with him, knowing he would always have good insight and advice. I thought about making love with him in bed at night and waking up in his arms in the morning. And I realized that even though we hadn't known each other very long and even though the logistics of building that kind of relationship with a man had always seemed impossible, I did want Micah Trains to be mine forever.

CHAPTER NINE

AT EIGHT o'clock the next evening I was standing in front of Micah's door with a bag of takeout and a serious case of nerves. After sharing meals and conversations for a week and then talking on the phone every night while he traveled during the next week, we were finally going to be alone together in private. There was no question in my mind that I would be sharing more than dinner with Micah that night. I knew he wanted me to share his bed, and I itched to do the same thing.

But wanting to do something so badly I could taste it wasn't the same thing as actually doing it. What if I wasn't any good? What if I tried to do something guys didn't do together? What if I got so nervous that I couldn't get it up? Okay, the last one didn't seem like a plausible concern given the current state of my dick.

No, y'all, that isn't a banana in my pocket. And it's not you I'm happy to see. *Ba-dum tsh*! Thank you very much, folks. I'm here all night. Please try the free-range, hormone free organic veal.

"Hey. Come on in." Micah stood next to his open door. He was wearing lightly distressed jeans, a heather-gray T-shirt, and no shoes.

I've never been one for feet. I mean, it's not like they gross me out or anything, I've just never given them any thought. But I found myself staring at Micah's feet and feeling my arousal ratchet up a notch or two. Great. Being gay wasn't enough. I had to have a weird fetish too. Honestly, I felt like a walking freak show.

Before I realized it, the door was slammed shut behind me, Micah's hand was around my waist pulling me toward him, and the takeout bag was on the floor. His lips covered mine with a hungry desperation. He licked and nibbled at my mouth while his fingers wove through my hair and held me close.

"You're so fuckin' hot, Ben. The way you look at me makes me nuts." He mumbled the words into my mouth and then kept kissing me, the fingers in my hair holding on and tugging. The small amount of pain combined with the pleasure from the kiss had me ready to come in my pants.

"What do you like?" he asked gruffly.

I didn't know how to answer that question. Sex had never been particularly great in my experience, at least not until I had made out with Micah in his pool. I was pretty sure the chlorine wasn't acting as an aphrodisiac. So if rubbing off against him had shattered my mind, anything else was likely to be just as good. But without ever having experienced the "anything else," I didn't know what to say.

When I didn't respond, Micah kept talking as he licked and nibbled his way across my jaw and down my neck. "Seriously, Ben. I can't keep my hands off you. I've been thinking about getting you naked for two weeks, and now that you're here, I don't think I can wait." One of his hands gripped the back of my neck, and the other trailed down my chest until he got to my waistband, and then he cupped my cock and gave it a squeeze. "Tell me what you're into. Other than feet, I mean. I got that one. Tell me what you want to do."

I was so turned on in that moment that I couldn't even work up a blush over the fact that he noticed me drooling over his feet. Plus, he didn't seem weirded out by it. If anything, the way he started mauling me before I even said hello indicated that he was turned on too.

"I want you. I'm into...anything," I replied. That seemed like a good answer, because given my state of excitement, Micah could have stood naked in front of me reciting the alphabet and I probably would have been stimulated enough to go off in my pants.

I felt Micah's hands on my ribcage and realized that he was pushing my T-shirt up my chest. Once he got it over my head, it landed on the floor and he peeled off his own shirt and then started working on my pants. When I looked around and noticed that we were in the hallway leading to his bedroom, I realized he had been moving us through the house while we were kissing and undressing.

"Damn. You're so perfect for me." He gave me a deep kiss and pushed my pants and briefs to the ground. I toed off my shoes and stepped out of the pants that were now pooled around my ankles. "I'm versatile too, but tonight I really want in here." He caressed my ass as he spoke, his fingers dipping into the crease.

I thought about saying no. Once I did this, I would never again be able to convince myself that I was straight. And if I couldn't convince myself, what chance did I have of convincing anybody else?

But really, that ship had already sailed. With or without sex, the intensity of my feelings for Micah Trains had already rung the death knell on that particular farce.

But plausible homosexual deniability aside, I'd had my hand on Micah's dick, and I knew the man wasn't lacking in the endowment department. The logistics of that particular body part going into a tight opening had always struck me as something that had to hurt. The thing was, though, I had been thinking about those logistics, because I had always wondered what it would feel like to have another man touch me that way. The idea that I could have a part of Micah inside me, that we could share such a primal, intimate connection, was so stimulating that I was willing to endure any pain— mental or physical—to experience it.

By the time I came to my decision, I was standing in Micah's bedroom, completely naked, while he shoved his pants and briefs to the floor. He leaned over me to get a grip on the comforter. Then he yanked it down and pulled me with him onto the bed.

"Oh, God! Micah!" I gasped when I felt his naked body press down onto mine.

The complete skin to skin contact with his hard frame felt incredible. We writhed together in an erotic dance of thrusting hips, groping hands, and gnawing mouths.

"Can't get enough of you," he moaned as he nipped at my shoulder and then my earlobe. "Want you so bad." He dragged his beard across my face, down my neck, and then he licked his way to my nipple. "Never felt like this before. It's crazy."

"Ungh!" I moaned when he bit my nipple and then soothed it with this tongue.

I hadn't realized that part of my body was particularly sensitive. But when Micah licked, sucked, and then bit my nipple, I arched off the bed and cried out in pleasure while I grasped his head and held him to my chest, begging him without words to continue.

"Love how responsive you are," he said and then gave a final lick to my left nipple before moving to my right and starting the delicious torture over again. He covered the hard nub with his mouth, sucked until I whimpered, and then released me and gently trailed his tongue over the now sensitive skin.

When my nipples were throbbing, he moved lower, his soft beard and wet tongue taking turns leading the journey over my ribcage and down my belly. When he reached my dick, Micah circled his big hand around it, held it out, and then rubbed his face over it. The sensation of the hair from his beard contrasted with that of his soft lips and wet tongue, which he darted out for an occasional swipe against my glans.

My head flew back, and I squeezed my eyes shut, trying to maintain control of my body. But the sound of Micah moaning in pleasure from the feeling of his face rubbing over my cock had my eyes flying open and staring at his erotic display. Never had anyone looked so turned on just from handling my dick. Seeing my wet crown move across Micah's cheek, recognizing the expression of bliss on his face, and hearing the groans streaming from him had me on the cusp of an orgasm.

Then he flattened his tongue and licked his way from the base of my dick to the crown and plunged down, taking my entire length into his mouth and throat. My hips bucked up and my hands grabbed the sides of his face. "Too good! Micah, I won't be able to stop..."

He popped off my cock and gazed up at me with those blue eyes blazing. "Fuck, I wanna taste your cum." He gave one last lick to my glans and then scrabbled to his knees and leaned over me. "But I think I want inside you more. Guess we'll have to save the other for round two."

He dropped a kiss onto my lips before he reached over to the nightstand, opened the drawer, and pulled out a condom and a bottle of lube. My heart was playing a high-speed game of badminton in my chest, and air wasn't quite filling my lungs. But none of that was because of nerves.

My hunger for Micah had taken over every aspect of my body and mind, which made succumbing to his silent cues come naturally. He opened the condom wrapper and covered his long, thick cock. Then he spread liquid onto his fingers, rubbed them together, and reached between my thighs. I instinctively spread my legs and canted my hips, opening myself to him as much as I could.

Wet, gentle strokes across my pucker had me whimpering with desire for more. Micah bent his face down over mine and kissed me gently as he pressed a finger inside my body. I couldn't hold back my gasp, but I concentrated on keeping my body relaxed.

"Shhh," he whispered to me. "You're so tight. Been a long time, huh? Don't worry; I'll take care of you."

He was so gentle, so kind. There was the confident-to-the-point-of-cocky Micah Trains, who could reduce hostile witnesses to tears and easily intimidate opposing counsel into defeat. And then there was my Micah—the funny, generous, tender lover who looked at me like I was the most precious thing he had ever seen. I blinked back tears from the emotions running rampant through me.

Micah's lips landed on mine once again, his tongue swept into my mouth, and another wet finger joined the first inside my body. The burn wasn't as noticeable the second time around. Then he twisted his hand, curled his fingers, and touched that spot inside me, and I was sure I would lose it. A thick bead of precum trickled down my impossibly hard cock.

"Feel good?" he asked in a soft, tender voice.

I nodded and leaned up to kiss him again. I couldn't get enough of his mouth, couldn't get enough of his tongue, couldn't get enough of him.

I felt him reaching for the bottle again, heard the click of the cap opening, and then a third slick digit entered my passage. My shoulders tensed, my hands clenched into fists, and I gasped for air. Micah licked a path down my neck and sucked on the spot where it met my shoulder.

"Nothing more until you're ready, Ben. I promise." He moved his fingers slowly in and out, turning them in one direction, then the other. "I haven't been with anyone in a long time either, more than a year. I'm not gonna rush this." He pushed in and found my prostate again, moving his fingertips back and forth over it until I was one big ball of desire.

"Micah, please." I could barely get the words out. "I need you." I reached up for a kiss, and he gave it to me, soft lips landing on mine. "Need you," I pleaded.

He nodded and pulled his fingers out, leaving me bereft. "I meant what I said the other day, you know." In that moment, I couldn't remember anything anyone had ever said. My entire being was centered on the smell of Micah's skin, the taste of Micah's tongue, and the feeling of that thick cock rubbing in circles across my entrance, preparing to take over my body. "I'm falling for you, Ben Forman."

He pushed into me slowly, breaking through the ring of muscle and not stopping until his cock was filling my passage and his balls were nestled against my ass. I looked up at him and gasped at the expression on his face. Nobody had ever looked at me that way, and even though I couldn't understand what a man like Micah Trains would see in me, the adoring gaze, the soft smile, and the sparkle in his eyes left no doubt in my mind. I had somehow lost my heart to Micah, but I wasn't alone in those feelings. He was right there with me.

He slowly dragged his dick out of my channel and then pushed it back in. I bent my knees and crossed my ankles over his back, then thrust my hips up and down to meet his pumps in and out of my body. Micah's hands searched for mine, and then he tangled our fingers together, dropped his forehead onto mine, and our bodies moved together toward completion.

Nothing had ever felt as good as Micah's dick pushing into me, Micah's stomach rubbing against my cock, and Micah's hands holding onto mine. His soft moans joined with my gasps and sighs of pleasure, and we continued moving, neither of us wanting the moment to end. But it was too good to last, and eventually Micah released one of my hands and snaked his hand between our bodies. He took hold of my cock and tugged on it as he increased the speed of his thrusts into my body.

"Come for me, Ben. Wanna see you lose it."

He pulled out until his crown was at my entrance, stretching me wide, and then he shoved back in with a powerful push angled to hit my gland. His hand joined his hips in the motion, and with a tight grip on my cock, he gave me a final stroke, and I cried out his name and sprayed my release across my stomach and chest.

"Yes, yes, God, yes!" Micah shouted with one more pump deep into my body. Then he held himself still and shuddered as he shot into the condom.

I wrapped my arms round Micah's back and pulled him down so his body was blanketing my own. He nestled his face in my neck, kissing and licking me as I pet his hair and neck.

"That was incredible, Ben," he sighed. "You're incredible." He pushed his upper body up and looked into my eyes with an unmatched tenderness.

My heart swelled. "It was the best ever." I hoped he realized that I meant it. I never knew sex could be like that, never knew anything could feel so good, never knew I could be so connected with another person. Like Micah said, it was incredible.

"Yeah?" he said, clearly pleased. "I'm glad, 'cause I really want to keep you coming back for more."

I smirked at him. "Well, you promised me round two, so I plan on coming more tonight."

Micah chuckled. "Count on it. But I think we both need

a little recovery time, so how about we take a little break and eat that dinner you brought over first?"

"Absolutely. My dick is a sweet treat, remember? And you can't eat your dessert until you finish your dinner." I tried to keep a straight face but failed miserably.

Micah shook his head and laughed. "That's not any funnier the second time around. Come on, let's go eat." He kissed my forehead and slid out of bed.

I watched his muscular globes move as he walked into the bathroom with that gait that made him look like he had just finished riding a horse. Or me. My groin tightened. Yeah, with Micah around as inspiration, recovery time didn't seem like an insurmountable issue.

CHAPTER TEN

MICAH HAD reached the bedroom door and I still hadn't moved out of bed. I was too distracted by his ass. He turned around and raised one eyebrow, his lips turning up in a cocky grin. "You can ogle me all you like in the kitchen. Let's go."

I forced myself to get out of bed and walk toward him. I assumed we would pick up the clothes we had dropped during our lust-filled groping session to the bedroom, but he just walked right past them and headed toward the kitchen.

"Wait. Aren't we getting dressed?" I asked.

He turned around and came back to me. Then he wrapped one arm around my waist and the other around my neck, pressing our nude torsos together. "It's just us, honey," he whispered into my ear. "You gonna get shy with me all of a sudden?"

I trembled in his arms and then immediately blushed. I was a strong, independent, grown man. Yet there was something about being with Micah that made me feel incredibly vulnerable. It seemed like he could see me, the real me, buried beneath all the façades I had put up over the years. I felt like I didn't have to be strong all the time, because maybe he could be strong enough for both of us. Letting go with Micah and letting myself be vulnerable felt incredibly freeing.

He must have taken my silence as an indication of discomfort with the naked eating plan, because he kissed my temple and pulled away. "I'll get you a pair of sweats to put on. Be right back."

I thought about telling him it was no big deal, but even when I was home alone, I made sure I was wearing pants and a shirt before I left my bedroom. That had been a rule growing up—no pants, no shirt, no walking through the house. I didn't even want to consider what my parents would have said if they'd caught us with bare skin in the kitchen.

Micah came back wearing a pair of worn gray sweats that barely clung to his hips, and nothing else. He handed me a navy pair and smiled. "I hate to cover up all that beauty, but I don't plan on spending too much time out here anyway." He dragged his eyes down my body as he spoke and gave me a lecherous smile.

I blushed again, took the pants, and pulled them on. The waist was a little snug on me, making me realize those sweats probably hung as loosely on Micah as the ones he was wearing, because his frame was narrower than mine, but otherwise they fit. I decided not to say anything about shirts. It wasn't as if there was any chance of my mother walking in and finding out we were half undressed around food.

Just the thought of my parents seeing me with Micah and realizing what we had been doing made me shudder and feel a little nauseous, but I forced myself to pull it together. And I thought I did a fine job of it, managing to keep the oh-my-God-what-have-I-done post-coital panic attack at bay, at least for a while.

Dinner was fun. We joked around, ate, played footsie under the table. Honestly, I had never even conceived of feeling so comfortable with someone, of laughing until my stomach hurt one minute and feeling so aroused that I wanted to maul him in the next. Add to that the fact that Micah was brilliant and incredibly successful and anybody with two brain cells to rub together would realize I had stumbled onto the perfect catch.

Do you happen to know anybody looking to sell a brain cell? 'Cause it looks like I'm one short.

When we finished eating, Micah stayed true to his word. He led me to the bedroom, pulled off my pants, and then licked his way down my body until his talented mouth reached my cock. After that it was Micah sucking and bobbing his head, me moaning and arching my ass off the bed, and then both of us coming—me deep in Micah's throat, and him kneeling above me, stroking himself, and shooting all over my chest.

He pulled the comforter up and curled himself around my body, nuzzling my neck. "I know it was just a week, but I missed you while I was out of town. I'd already gotten used to spending time with you every day." He leaned up, kissed my cheek, and locked his eyes with mine. "I'm so glad you're here with me now."

I wanted to tell him that I had missed him too. I wanted to say that I was gladder to be with him than I had any business being. But the words didn't come out, and then I was asleep.

My norm before finally falling asleep most nights was at least an hour or two of mental flogging and self-recrimination over all the ways I wasn't measuring up to my parents' expectations, or my potential, or anything else I could come up with. But that night, I slept soundly, my limbs tangled with Micah's, his scent surrounding me. It was wonderful.

I HAD an hour-long commute to and from work, so my body was used to waking up early. Not realizing it was a Saturday, my bladder gave me a wakeup call before dawn. It was dark in Micah's bedroom, but even in my half-asleep, foggy state, I managed to make it into the bathroom without crashing into anything and waking him up. As tired as I knew he was from his trip, he was probably dead to the world anyway.

I flipped the light on, made my way around the bathroom, and then stopped at the sink to wash my hands. My brain was still fuzzy with sleep, so I wasn't thinking clearly. I looked at myself in the mirror and saw my body in distinct snapshots. Reddened nipples. Love bites on my chest. White, crusty dried release on my stomach. I clenched my ass and felt the unfamiliar sensation of skin and muscle that had been touched and used for the first time. Almost as if it were connected by a wire, my dick immediately began filling.

What was wrong with me? I looked like I had been ravished. Hell, I had been ravaged. I had lain in that bed and let a man have complete dominion over me, over even the most intimate parts of my body. That shouldn't be a turn-on. I was stronger than that. I had to be.

Hello, Mister Morning-After Regret. I didn't realize you came to visit when no alcohol was involved, but I'm not surprised you made a special exception for me.

I stumbled out of the bathroom, hurried through the house, and gathered my clothes. Two minutes later, I was outside, walking barefoot to my car, with my socks and shoes in my hand and an emptiness I refused to acknowledge forming in my chest.

My intention was to drive home, scrub myself clean, and find a way to get my life under control. So I was surprised when I found myself parked in front of my brother's house. I mean, yeah, I had driven there and everything, so it shouldn't have been a shocker. But there it was.

Well, as long as I was there, I might as well stop in to say hello. I wasn't in his neighborhood all that often, after all, and it would be rude to just leave without... Whatever, I needed help, and my subconscious had taken me to my brother's house. Good to know part of me was still capable of making a rational decision. I put my shoes on without bothering with socks, put one foot in front of the other, and rang Noah's doorbell.

It took a while for him to answer, and when he finally did, I coughed and looked down. Noah was stark naked, glaring at me. "What the fuck, Ben? Is someone dead?"

"Huh?" I asked intelligently.

"It's six in the morning," he grumbled, but then he stepped aside and waved his arm back and forth. "Come in, come in."

I walked into his house and moved toward the family room on autopilot, settling into the corner of the couch. "Sorry. I forgot how early it is. Did I wake you guys up?"

"It's fine. Clark's still asleep, and I'll catch a nap later." He settled into the armchair across from me and stretched his long legs in front of him, completely comfortable in his own skin.

How had we grown up in the same house? I couldn't conceive of sitting on furniture naked. My father's disapproving voice was practically shouting in my head just from the thought of it.

I know, I know. My parents spend way too much time in my head. I need help.

Look, I was trying, okay? I wasn't perfect, far from it, but I really was trying.

I gathered my courage and looked at my brother. "I

have a question."

"Ninety-six." His face was completely expressionless.

"What?"

"You said you had a question," he responded. "And I gave you an answer. Ninety-six. Make it work."

That was usually the point in a conversation with my brother where I gave up and changed the topic to sports or work or the weather. But this was too important for me to give up, so I forced myself to drudge forward. "Can you please try to take me seriously for once? I think something's wrong with me, Noah, and I don't know how to fix it."

I folded my arms over my knees and dropped my face down, trying to guard myself from his reaction. He was quiet for a long time, longer than I thought possible with my outspoken brother. Then I heard him sigh before he started talking. "There's nothing wrong with you that you can't fix. I'm just spit-ballin' here, but maybe if you just stopped fuckin' hiding and pretending to be someone you're not, well maybe then you wouldn't be so damn miserable all the time."

I looked up at him and wondered how he knew how unhappy I had been for so long. I thought I had been doing such a good job hiding my feelings under a plastic smile and carefree demeanor. "What if what I am is...broken or wrong, somehow?"

What if what I am will disappoint our parents? I didn't ask that question because I knew how little our parents' opinions mattered to him. Besides, processing the sex from the previous night was enough of a challenge to address in one conversation.

"Look, Ben, I'm not a mind reader. Tell me what's going on with you. Just say it. I seriously doubt you're as fucked up as you seem to think. And if you are, well, you know I won't pull any punches."

That was true. If I could count on Noah for one thing, it was raw honesty. I plunged ahead. "I met someone. A guy." I looked at the floor and noticed my foot tapping restlessly.

"Better late than never," Noah said under his breath.

I shook my head. "You don't understand. When I'm with him, I can't...I don't know. I can't think straight or something."

He chuckled. "What's the problem here? Seems to me you're finally heading in the right direction. Thinking straight's been the issue all along."

I looked my brother in the eyes, imploring him to understand and not make fun of me. "He did things to me, and I let him," I blurted out.

Noah's expression hardened immediately. "He hurt you?" He got up and walked over to me, looking over my face and body slowly. "Who is he? What'd he do to you? I'll fuckin' kill him."

Noah was younger than me, but he was bigger, stronger, and generally angrier, which made him a formidable opponent. I should know, because I was usually on the receiving end of his threats, and then some. That was the first time in my entire life that my brother had been protective of me or expressed any sort of concern over my well-being. I was shocked and pleased in equal parts, so it took me a few moments to answer. Eventually, I shook my head. "No, it wasn't like that. That's what I'm trying to tell you. I wanted him to do those things."

The tension left his shoulders, and he sat next to me on the couch. "What, like he spanked you or tied you up or something?"

I gasped and shook my head. "No! Nothing that awful. Jesus, do people actually do sick things like that?" Sex talk with my friends had always been about women with particularly big tits or maybe flexible bodies. Bondage had never entered the equation. "Maybe you're right. If there are actually people messed up enough to do that shit, then I guess I'm better off than I thought."

Noah got up from the couch and walked back over to his chair, dragging his fingers through his hair in a clear display of frustration. "You're a special kind of stupid, aren't you, Ben?"

And the normal Noah was back. I wondered how I could have concerned-brother Noah hang around for just a little bit longer. "What I'm trying to tell you is..." I swallowed hard and shut my eyes for a couple of seconds before I found the courage to continue. "When we were together, I wasn't the guy, you know?"

"You weren't the guy?" Noah looked like he was

barely containing a smirk.

"Come on, Noah, don't make me say it. You know what I mean."

"Yeah, I know what you mean, Ben. But you're both guys. That's the whole point, and what you do with each other in bed doesn't change that." He took a deep breath, seemingly trying to rein in his usual verbal attacks. "Let's just move on. Did you get off on it?"

My blush seemed to be all the answer he needed.

"Okay, I think I've got the picture. You met a guy and hit it off. You had sex, good sex if the look on your face right now is any indication, but every silver lining has a cloud, and you've managed to find it. So now you're freaking out because you bottomed and liked it."

"Bottomed" wasn't a term I had previously heard, but I understood it in context. I was glad Noah was on the same page. Maybe he could help me. "Yes, that's what happened."

"Look, Ben, if you go twelve rounds with a punching bag, the punching bag always wins." Great, a kickboxing analogy. Do you have any idea what he meant? I sure didn't. He rolled his eyes and dumbed it down for me. "You're always going to be unhappy if you insist on finding every reason possible to hate yourself. It's normal to be a little freaked out about sex at first. I mean, I wasn't, but there are some guys who have a lot of macho bullshit going on about being on the receiving end."

He shrugged, and I bit my tongue to keep myself from

saying something snarky about him never having freaked out about sex. Of course he hadn't. It was all so simple for Noah, yet the morning-after anxiety was well on its way to putting me in an early grave. It seemed like everything made sense in my brother's mind. I wanted that kind of peace. I let my head fall onto the back of the couch and covered my eyes with my forearm.

"So you don't think it makes me less of a man if I liked it when he...when he..." I stammered but couldn't complete the sentence.

"No," he said simply. I sat up straight and blinked my eyes open, wanting very much to hear his opinion. My brother's expression was softer than usual. "I say, if it's good, keep doing it, you know? But if you're not into it, then don't. Some guys are strict tops, some guys don't get into ass play at all. Different strokes and all that. The point is being real, being you, and not hiding anymore. You should do whatever gets you hot, Ben, and if that means being a bottom or being versatile, well, that's what it means." He shrugged. "What we do in bed doesn't define our masculinity."

Could it be that easy? I had enjoyed being with Micah the previous night, really enjoyed it. Was that a sufficient justification to keep doing it? "I really like him, Noah. I mean, I *really* like him."

"I can tell. Does he feel the same way about you?"

I thought about how Micah looked at me when we were together. Wherever we were—in a restaurant, in the office, at his house—he seemed completely focused on me, and his gaze was always so tender. He made me feel as if I was the center of his world.

I nodded. "Yeah, I think he does. I have no idea why, but I think he's just as into me."

Noah smirked. "That's good, 'cause based on the wrinkled clothes, dreadful bedhead, the ungodly hour of this visit, I'm guessing you had sex with him, freaked out, and then snuck out of the house in the middle of the night."

I felt the blood drain from my face. "Oh, shit."

CHAPTER ELEVEN

ALL RIGHT, so I had already blown it with Micah once when I had acted like an ass during that whole botched coffee run thing. And now I had slinked out of his house while he was still asleep after we'd had sex for the first time. How many strikes did I get in this game before I was out of his life?

Walking out on someone in bed without a word or at least a note was a shitty thing to do. So shitty, in fact, that I had never done it no matter how much I hadn't wanted to see a woman again. Leave it to me to start with the one person I actually wanted to see first thing in the morning. And every moment after that.

It was early, so I hoped that maybe Micah was still asleep and I could crawl back into bed without him ever knowing I had left. Just the thought of his warm, naked body pressed against mine had my pulse racing. I was about to turn down his street when I realized that the door locked behind me and I didn't have a key.

Since breaking and entering wasn't an option, I threw plan A out the window and drove to the first bagel place I could find. Plan B would be bagels and coffee. Strike that, bagels and tea. I could be considerate went-to-get-you-breakfast guy instead of mentally-unbalanced-had-a-hissy-fit-and-slithered-out-like-a-snake guy.

During the drive back to Micah's place, I made little bargains with myself. If I didn't hit any red lights, he would still be sleeping and wouldn't know I had snuck off. If I made it to the next corner before the clock changed to the next minute, he wouldn't be pissed at me. If I remembered all the words to the song on the radio, things would turn out fine.

Despite what you're probably thinking right now, I was thirty-one, not twelve. But I was also a little OCD, and being a baseball nut came with a predisposition to being superstitious. Plus—and I'm not gonna lie to you about this because, let's face it, I'm sure you already figured it out—I'm batshit crazy. On the credit column, though, I have a great ass and a nice smile, a combination that's been known to compensate for a lot of personality flaws.

I sure as hell hoped it would be enough with Micah, because I got stuck at every red light on the way there, and not once did I make it to a corner within the minute timeline I had set. Oh, and they were playing a Nirvana marathon on the radio. Great band, legendary, even, but don't even try to pretend that you can decipher Kurt Cobain's mumbling.

When I got back to Micah's house, I knocked quietly and held my breath as I awaited my fate. It took him a long time to answer the door. I took that as an indication that he was still sleeping, which was great. I mean, I felt bad about waking him up and everything, but if he was asleep, then my cover would work and he would never have to know about my embarrassing morning episode.

"Hey." He stood in front of the open door, rubbing the back of his neck with his right hand. The same sweatpants I had worn the night before were barely hanging on his hips, and he didn't have anything else on. Damn, was he ever gorgeous.

None of the lights were on in the entryway or the adjoining living room, and a wave of relief washed over me. He had just woken up and I was safe. I smiled at him and walked inside, stopping to lean in for a kiss. He hesitated, which I thought was strange, but then he moved his hand from his nape to the back of my head and drew me to him, nibbling on my lower lip before pulling away.

"I went to get breakfast," I said as I held up the box of bagels in one hand, the drink carrier in the other.

He furrowed his brow and chewed on his bottom lip for a second. Then he reached for the drinks and started walking toward the kitchen. "That's perfect. I don't have anything to eat in the house because I always clean out my fridge before I go on business trips, and I didn't have time to go to the grocery store yesterday."

I felt the remains of the tension leave my body. Everything had worked out just fine. I'd had a really good talk with my brother for what might have been the first time in my life, I was a hero for bringing in food, and Micah didn't know about my momentary lapse of reason and decency.

Total hat trick. Go me.

When we got to the kitchen, Micah got a couple of plates out of the cabinet and a knife out of the drawer. "Did you happen to pick up some cream cheese? I think I have that spreadable not-really-butter stuff and a jar of jelly, but that's about it."

I laughed. "Don't worry, I gotcha covered." I held up the cream cheese container. "You weren't kidding about throwing everything out before traveling, were you?"

"It's a lesson learned the hard way after I came back from a trip that lasted longer than expected and ate what I thought was blue cheese," he replied with a wince. "While it technically had some blue-green parts, it had started out as Colby, which I didn't realize until I was sick as a dog a little while later."

I laughed. "You couldn't tell old Colby from blue cheese?"

He came over to me and circled his arms around my waist. Damn, but did it feel good to have him touch me. I rubbed my cheek against his beard and then turned into his neck, resting against his shoulder. He rubbed circles on my back and kissed my forehead.

"Hey, it was late. I was tired and jet-lagged. I just wanted to eat something and crawl into bed, and I wasn't paying all that much attention to what it was."

I nodded as I lifted my head up and looked at him.

Micah took a long breath, and then he cupped my

cheek and stroked my lip with his thumb. "Late night snacks aside, though, I pay a lot of attention to what happens in my bed. It's not something I take lightly. I hope you know that."

As Micah's words sank in, my eyes landed on the kitchen table. His laptop was open, a case file was spread out around it, and an empty mug was sitting next to it. None of those things had been there when we had eaten dinner the previous night.

My head jerked back to look at Micah. He hadn't been sleeping. From the look of things, I guessed he had probably woken up not long after I had left. No way did he believe it took me over an hour to pick up bagels from a place down the street.

My heart slammed against my ribcage as I tried to figure out what to say. Micah leaned forward and kissed the tip of my nose. Then he moved over and turned away as he started digging through the box on the counter. "Did you get savory or sweet? Oh, a mix of both. Perfect."

I came up behind him and pressed my chest to his back, wrapping my arms around him and giving him a tight squeeze. Grateful didn't begin to express how I felt about him letting me off the hook without demanding an explanation. I kissed the back of his neck. "Perfect's just the right description," I mumbled against his warm skin.

I meant it. I really, really meant it. It was the crap I spewed a few weeks later that I didn't actually mean.

MICAH HAD a case scheduled to go to trial in mid-September. To say he was working hard through the end of April and early May was an understatement. But it seemed as if he spent every free moment with me. Because of his long hours at the office every day, he didn't really have time to go out, so we had been spending our free time at his place. Usually we would pick up some takeout on the way out of the office or throw together a quick dinner in his gourmet kitchen and catch up on our days while we ate.

It was incredibly domestic, which amazed me. Yes, I had a gay brother. And yes, he had been in a committed relationship with the same man forever. But spending time with Noah and Clark together was a relatively new phenomenon for me, and my brain was still processing the realization that my fears about what being gay would mean—loneliness, indiscriminate screwing around, partying all night, body glitter (okay, the last one was a secret wish on my part; don't tell anyone)—weren't really true. Or at least they didn't have to be true. Strangely, my relationship with a man had already lasted longer and felt more settled than what I'd had with any ex-girlfriend.

And that doesn't even get into the sex. Dear God, the sex. No matter how tired Micah was at the end of each day, he always found the energy to attack me when we got into bed. Actually, there were a few nights when he didn't even wait that long.

I had come in his entryway when he pressed me against the front door, shoved his hand down my pants, and tugged on my cock as he stabbed his tongue into my mouth. I had come in his living room when he put his laptop on the coffee table, took the remote control and muted the baseball game, and then dropped to his knees and went down on me. And, in a move that would have seriously made my parents lose their shit, I had come in his kitchen, pressed against the counter, with Micah draped over my back pushing deep into my body.

Despite the long hours working, our relationship was flourishing on every level. And the happiness and peace I found with Micah permeated every aspect of my life. Work was going well. I had been getting along with my brother and Clark. The time I spent with my parents was bearable because I always knew I would get to see Micah as soon as it was over. Basically, everything was going great.

So of course I had to fuck it up.

IT WAS Sunday afternoon, and we were at Micah's place watching a Glory game. Well, I was watching baseball. Micah was alternately watching and reading a deposition transcript in preparation for his trial.

He was sitting at the end of the couch, his feet resting on the ottoman, his right hand holding the document, and his left hand petting my hair. I was lying across the couch with my head pillowed on his lap. It was relaxing, and I found my eyes dropping closed every so often, but I couldn't quite fall asleep.

I decided the problem was my unattended erection. The crazy thing about really frequent, really great sex was that it made me hornier. I've already mentioned that sex hadn't been a big thing for me before Micah. I mean, sleeping with women didn't really get me going because...yeah, okay, you've already figured that one out. Anyway, I had always liked beating off, and I had done it regularly. But by no means had I ever gotten hard as often, or needed to come as desperately, as I had since I had gotten together with Micah.

We had already fooled around that morning before we got out of bed and I had no doubt he would take care of me again that night. Still, I found myself wiggling around, unable to get comfortable and wanting to turn my head so my face was buried in his lap and I could inhale his scent. My mouth watered with the thought of his taste.

Damn! When had I become so needy? I had always been fine on my own. I mean, yeah, I had kept girlfriends around, but that was just for events or group dates. I rarely spent time alone with them, and when I did, I was fine when we went our separate ways after a couple of hours. I forced myself to get up and walk into the kitchen, hoping some distance would help me put things in perspective.

What was it about Micah that made boring, everyday things more enjoyable when I was with him? I downed a bottle of water, paced, and cracked my knuckles. Then I peered around the corner to look at Micah sitting on the couch, chewing on the end of a highlighter and running a hand over his beard.

He looked so intense when he was concentrating on work. It reminded me of his expression when he looked at me sometimes, like I was important, like I meant something. I found myself walking toward him on autopilot, just wanting to get a little closer.

Knowing he was busy, I approached the back of the couch so I wouldn't distract him. He set the paper and highlighter down on the end table and reached his hand over his shoulder. "C'mere, honey."

I walked over and rubbed his shoulders, trying to massage away some of his tension. I knew how important the case was. Half our firm had been working on it since things started heating up. A good outcome for the client would be great for all of us, especially Micah, since he was the lead attorney. "I didn't mean to interrupt you. I know you're busy."

He covered my hand with his, turned his face, and then brought my hand to his mouth and kissed my palm. "Mmm. Not too busy for you."

I draped both arms over his shoulders and caressed my way down his bare chest, enjoying the feeling of hard muscles under my hands. By the time I got to his waistband, his head was leaning back against the couch, his eyes were closed, and his expression was nothing short of blissful. I took that as encouragement and unbuttoned his jeans, letting my hands slide in and stroke his hard cock while I leaned over and kissed his neck.

"Feels so good, honey. Love the way you touch me," he murmured softly.

I continued stroking his cock, keeping my pace steady and my grip firm but not too tight. Micah turned his head and met my lips, kissing me, nibbling and tugging on my bottom lip and occasionally darting his tongue out and taking a taste. When my left hand joined the party and cupped his balls, Micah's hips shot off the couch.

"Damn, Ben, that's good. Yeah, just like that. Roll 'em in your hand."

So I did. I rubbed his balls, squeezing and rolling them, stroked his cock, and peppered his face with kisses. And it wasn't long before I was rewarded with a triumphant shout and wet heat pouring onto my hand.

My desire to taste Micah had me acting without any thought. I brought my cum-coated hand to my mouth and licked his seed off. Oh, damn, the taste of him turned me on even more. I closed my eyes and moaned.

"Ahh, shit. Get over here." Micah's voice sounded like

it was being dragged over gravel.

He turned around, grasped my waist, and encouraged me to move around to the front of the couch. When I was standing in front of him, he made quick work of my button and zipper, and before I knew it, my pants and briefs were at my ankles and my cock was lodged in Micah's throat.

The man sucked like he was on a mission, a swiping tongue, a tight seal of his lips around my dick, and hard pulls as he bobbed back and forth. His hands made their way to my ass, and he pulled me forward, encouraging me to move and pump into him. I clasped his shoulder with one hand and the back of his head with the other as I plunged in and out of his warm, welcoming mouth.

"Micah. So good, so good," I rambled unintelligently as my orgasm neared. The hands on my ass held me tighter and spread me apart, exposing my rosebud. Then long fingers dipped into my crack and rubbed over that sensitive spot.

"Yes!" I cried out. "Want you inside."

I rocked against him, hoping he would give me what I needed. I shouldn't have worried. Micah had never left me hanging. He pushed one long finger into me and increased the pace of his sucks, inspiring a knee-buckling orgasm. I shot down his throat and called out his name before I collapsed onto his lap and rested my head on his shoulder.

CHAPTER TWELVE

MICAH RUBBED circles on my stomach and kissed my forehead as my post-orgasm pulse slowed to a normal rate and I caught my breath. I snuggled into his embrace, resting my head on his shoulder and nuzzling his neck. "You make me feel amazing," I whispered.

He tightened his hold on me. "The feeling's mutual."

We sat quietly together, just sharing soft touches and enjoying each other's presence. But I knew he had work to do, so eventually I sat up. "Sorry for distracting you. I need to visit my parents today. I'll be out of your hair and you can get some more work done."

Getting away with seeing my parents less frequently was one thing. Saying no to Sunday dinner after I had made excuses for why I was out of pocket all week was something else. If I tried to pull that move, I would be subjected to pursed lips and disapproving looks for months.

"I'm actually pretty caught up. I mean, there's always more to do on this fuckin' case, but if you want me to..." Micah hesitated. His hand, which had been rubbing my chest, paused. "If you want us to go somewhere today, I can."

There really wasn't anywhere I wanted to go. Being

at Micah's house meant privacy, which worked out great for me. As long as it was just the two of us, everything was wonderful. I got to be with him without anyone finding out that I was with a guy and without said guy finding out I was a chickenshit. Win-win as far as I was concerned. Plus, I didn't have time to go anywhere that day. I needed to go to my place, do some laundry, and eat dinner with my parents.

"No worries. I have dinner with my parents today anyway." I sat up and kissed his cheek. "Actually, I need to get going. Even with light Sunday traffic, the drive takes forever."

When I stood, Micah rubbed the nape of his neck, a move I had come to realize meant he was frustrated about something. "Yeah, I know. And like I said, I'm fine taking a break from work if you want me to go *anywhere* with you."

That was when his meaning hit me. He wanted to come with me to dinner at my parents' house. Was he out of his mind? What possible excuse could I use to explain why I was bringing a buddy to Sunday dinner? If we went there together, they could figure out what we had been up to.

My eyes widened as realization dawned. That was exactly what he wanted. He thought I would introduce him to my parents as my...my what? The man I'd been screwing? They were the last people on earth I would grace with that information. Hell, Clark had been a regular fixture at our house for years before my parents found out about him and Noah. But as soon as they'd realized he wasn't just a friend or roommate, he had become persona non grata, no longer welcome at dinners or holidays or anything else. And because my brother refused to go where Clark wasn't welcome, that had been the death knell in their relationship with Noah too.

How could Micah expect me to choose him over my family? Things were fine as they were. I spent more time with him than I had with any girlfriend. The sex was good—amazing, even. It was enough. Why did he need to push me for more?

"I've gotta go," I mumbled as I stalked out of the room.

The clothes I had worn that weekend were in Micah's bedroom, folded on a chair in the corner. I stuffed my feet into my shoes, gathered my wallet, clothes, and keys, and turned toward the bedroom doorway.

Micah was leaning on the doorframe, his arms crossed over his firm chest, a concerned expression painted on his uniquely handsome face. I refused to feel guilty about not inviting him to dinner. Hell, my mother could get a job as a travel agent with the skill she exhibited putting guilt trips together. Micah had nothing on her. And if she found out what we had been doing, if my father found out... I shook my head.

No. Just no. I couldn't do that to them, couldn't stomach the look of disappointment on their faces, couldn't leave them without a relationship with either of their children. I forced myself to keep an even expression on my face as I approached the doorway and Micah standing in it.

He put his hand on my shoulder and looked into my eyes. "Come on. Don't do this again, Ben."

All attempts at holding in my feelings evaporated, and I exploded, shouting at him. "Do what? What do you want from me? I say I'm having dinner with my parents and you get all pouty. I don't appreciate the pressure, Micah. It's too much. I think I'll stay at my place tonight. Maybe some time apart will help you start acting like a man and not a little girl."

Yeah, I know. You're thinking I'm a total asshole. Or maybe a dumb shit. Oh, a fucktard? That sounds about right. Hey, it's what I do. I really know how to make the worst of a good situation. It's a special talent. What can I say?

He gasped, dropped his hand from my shoulder, sucked his lower lip into his mouth, and squeezed his eyes closed. There was a part of me that itched to take it all back, to drop the things I was holding on the floor and wrap my arms around his chest. But the bigger part of me was scared, terrified even.

I wasn't lying when I said it was all too much. Being with Micah was wonderful, no question about it. But having people find out about us meant giving up so many things. My parents would be devastated, and if the fallout from my brother's coming out was any indication, our relationship would be irreparably ruined. My circle of friends would never understand. They all had wives or girlfriends. How could I explain my failure to make that work in my own life?

And what about work? The way Micah talked, I gathered he didn't hide who he was. I had decided the only reason he wasn't fodder for the gossip mill was because he was single, so people hadn't figured it out. But even if they did, he was so highly regarded he would be fine. I didn't have that luxury. I hadn't been practicing as long, didn't have his unparalleled reputation, didn't have the same client base...it was just different for me.

The bottom line was that being with Micah meant I couldn't be the same man I had always been. And that scared me. So off I went, leaving Micah's house in a tizzy (again). I got in my car and drove home, refusing to change my mind, refusing to feel regretful, refusing to think at all.

IT MAY have turned out differently if I hadn't had so damn much experience burying myself in the sand. It wasn't just my head. I would do a full body submerging and stay there, sometimes for years at a time. Well, I didn't hide for years that time. I couldn't. I missed Micah too much. But the week I spent avoiding him was damaging enough.

I didn't go back to his house that Sunday and I didn't take his call when it came in that night. On Monday, I pointedly avoided eye contact and ignored his disappointed sigh when he came into the kitchen at work to get a bottle of water just as I was walking out with yet another coffee, trying to stay awake after a restless night. Tuesday and Wednesday, I closed my office door and refused to come out other than for a couple of much-needed bathroom breaks that consisted of me scurrying to the bathroom like a rat in the hopes of not being detected.

Look, if you think you're clever with the whole "you are a rat, Ben" thing, you're not. I thought it too. But I wasn't ready to do anything about it yet. It took two more days before I internally slapped myself around (I know you were hoping for something that would actually leave bruises) and crawled out of the hole I had dug for myself.

Damn it! I missed him. I missed the way he growled under his breath when was reading a particularly annoying document. I missed the way he chewed on his bottom lip and furrowed his brow when he was thinking of the answer to a Trivial Pursuit question. I missed the way his eyes shone when he looked at me. I missed how he bumped his hip against mine when we cooked dinner together, and then dropped a kiss on my cheek or lips. I just missed him.

I knew that feeling wasn't going to go away. So I could either sit and sulk about how it was all his fault for pushing me for too much too fast, or I could go talk to him. In a long overdue display of maturity, I chose the latter and showed up on Micah's doorstep on Saturday afternoon.

When he answered the door, all the anxiety and frustration that had been consuming me for close to a week had to vacate to make room for a whole new type of pain.

There wasn't even a trace of the smile that had always graced Micah's face when he saw me. The sparkle in his eyes was gone. And he didn't reach for me, not for a hello kiss, not for a hug, not for anything.

"Hi, Ben." That strong hand that had touched every part of my body with tenderness and passion cupped the nape of his neck.

"Hi." I shifted from foot to foot, nerves suddenly striking me mute.

"Do you want to come in?" he asked.

I nodded, and he stepped aside, leaving me a wide berth to walk into his house. He closed the door behind me and walked into the living room, taking a seat in the arm chair and waiting for me to join him. I sat on the couch and twisted my fingers together, focusing on my hands instead of his face.

It took a good three minutes of complete silence before I realized he wasn't going to just brush this under the rug and move on. I didn't have much experience with talking out issues. My parents were more the silent disapproving types. My brother usually just attacked and screamed. And as far as relationships went, I had always been the disposable boyfriend type—when something went wrong, I would end it or she would end it, and that was that. So knowing how to fix things after a fight was a completely foreign concept. "I'm sorry," I said.

There. That should work, right? I apologized.

"For what?" he asked, peering at me with those blue eyes that had once been filled with affection and arousal but now remained completely flat.

Jesus! If that wasn't a loaded question, I didn't know what was. I was sorry for so many things it was impossible to list them. My entire existence felt like cause for an apology.

"I don't..." I paused and cleared my throat before continuing. "I'm sorry for yelling at you last week. I'm sorry for what I said. I didn't mean it."

Micah rested his forearms on his knees and clasped his hands together. He looked down for several long seconds before finally lifting his gaze to meet mine. "So then why did you say those things, Ben? What happened to set you off? We were having a nice morning. Everything seemed fine. And then you just exploded, stormed out, and shut down. You've been avoiding and ignoring me for a week. I felt like I was being punished for something, and I didn't understand what it was."

I answered before thinking. Not a good move on my part, clearly, but I was a hella slow learner.

"I overreacted. I get that now. It's just that you were acting like I should be introducing you to my parents. Like it was a given that we'd be going to their house together." I probably should have stopped talking then, but I kept going, giving myself more rope. "And you're always like that. All confident, acting like we're a couple. I don't remember you asking me if that was what I wanted. You just assumed. Like it's a given that I'd want the same thing."

He flinched and then sighed. "I see."

"What does that mean?" My voice squeaked when I asked the question, and I hated myself just a little bit more for sounding like a little kid. Right, as if it was the squeak that created that effect.

"It means that I'm too old and tired to keep going with this"—he waved his hand back and forth between us— "whatever we have going."

Nothing frustrates me more than the moment during an argument when I realize I'm wrong. Yeah, I hadn't spoken to Micah in almost a week, but I hadn't been thinking during that time, hadn't allowed myself the option of thinking. And as I sat there looking at Micah Trains, I realized that being with him was what I wanted. I did want us to be a couple. And I knew he wanted it too. Why was he playing games with me?

"Oh, come on, Micah, don't try to pretend like you're not into me. I've been there this past month, okay? You get off hard when we're together and we both know it. You said you're falling for me, and I know it's true. I can tell from the way you look at me. You're into me."

Micah stood up and started pacing back and forth across the room. "What's going on here, Ben? Are you waiting for me to pretend like the sex wasn't good? Or am I supposed to act like I don't enjoy spending time with you? Or maybe you think I'm denying my feelings? Well, that's your bag, not mine. Yeah, the sex was hot. Yeah, I have fun with you. I think you're smart. I think you're interesting. And I like you, Ben. A lot."

He paused to glare at me, his hand making its way to the customary spot on the nape of his neck.

"So then why are you walking away?" I asked in a whisper.

His hands flew into the air. "I'm walking away because I can't build a life with a guy who thinks that me having feelings for him is a character flaw or something I should be embarrassed about. I'm not a kid, Ben. I'm almost forty years old, and I'm done with the playing around shit. I've been done with it for years." He slumped into his chair and lowered his voice. "Look, I'm not looking for a good lay to share my bed for a night. I'm looking for a good man to share my entire life. And no matter how much I like you, no matter how much I wish you could be that guy, Ben, we both know you're not."

I was desperate by that point. I was losing Micah and I couldn't figure out how to stop it, how to hang on to the person who had come to mean so much to me. I couldn't go back to my old life. I didn't want to be that guy anymore, even if it made my parents happy, even if it made my clients happy. I hated that version of me. Panic does not make for effective negotiating.

"Why can't I be that guy? Because I'm not falling at your feet and saying whatever you want, suddenly it's over?"

He sighed deeply, and I could see regret and disappointment in his expression. "No, because I have no interest in being with someone who gets off on leaving me unbalanced. Look, you either want to be with me or you don't. I was hoping you did, but if not, I'll live. That doesn't mean I'll be happy about it. I'm not pretending it won't suck. But I'll live. What I won't do, though, is stay around so you can withhold your affection or your commitment or whatever the hell you're trying to withhold to make some point I don't understand. If you want me, Ben, then fucking want me and own it. Don't give me shit because I'm confident about your feelings. You should want me to be fucking confident about them. Because if you care about someone, you want them to feel good, to feel safe. And if you don't, well, that's okay, too, but I'm not in the market for a fuck buddy."

CHAPTER THIRTEEN

I WON'T drag you down by describing every detail of the next couple of weeks, but believe me when I tell you that they were hell. I kept up an upbeat, positive public front. I'd had a lifetime of experience pretending to be happy-go-lucky guy, after all, so keeping up that persona was second nature. But inside...inside I couldn't find a way to snap out of my funk and get myself together.

After Micah ended things with me, I left his house in a daze. I don't remember driving back to my condo or walking up the stairs. I don't remember the next couple of days. It was only when my secretary called me on Tuesday morning to ask whether I was still sick that I realized I had missed work on Monday. I made it to the office after that, but I found myself reading the same paragraph over and over again and refusing to answer any telephone calls.

On Friday afternoon, I happened to walk by Micah's office on the way to... Fine, I didn't have any legitimate reason to walk by; I just wanted to catch a glimpse of him. Please stop patting yourself on the back. Guessing that little piece of humiliating information isn't all that insightful. I mean, it's pretty clear by this point to anyone with even basic reading comprehension that I was a complete basket case. Anyway, I walked by his office and heard him talking on the phone.

He sounded levelheaded and articulate. The point he was making to the caller was logical and well researched. The man was brilliant and completely on top of his game. And that fucking pissed me off.

How could he be so perfectly fine when I was such a mess? Hadn't I meant anything to him? Had he been lying when he said he was falling for me?

Well, I didn't need him anyway. I had been fine before him (yeah, total crap, I know, but I wasn't being very rational at that moment), and I would be fine after him. I just needed to dust myself off and go back to the way things had been before Micah Trains had swaggered into my life.

Now, item number one of my pre-Micah life agenda had always been to find a girlfriend. After that, I could go to a show or a party or any kind of event with her. That would be better than staying at home and continuing my mission of creating a permanent Ben-sized sofa indentation.

Although I preferred setups, I didn't have that kind of time to invest in finding a girlfriend. So after work on Friday, I went to a nice bar downtown. There'd be plenty of women there for happy hour at the end of the week. Finding one to date for a little while wouldn't be an issue.

That whole fiasco lasted about two hours. Yes, there were plenty of women at the bar. Nice women. Smart women. Pretty women. But they were *women*, and my body staunchly refused to play another round of Hide in the Closet.

I'm not sure what made me drive to a gay bar. I left the bar downtown, wondering what I was going to do with my life (not night, *life*). There was no energy left in me to pretend any longer. I remembered a gay bar that I had driven by many times on the way to my brother's house, so I drove to EC West.

At first, I was nervous about being in a gay bar. I stayed on the perimeter of the space in the darkest shadows I could find, just scoping things out. Odds were that would have been the end of it. I mean, realistically, I didn't have the balls to go out there and pick up someone with, well, balls. But as it turned out, I didn't need to make any sort of effort.

Much to my surprise, a guy approached me. He chatted me up for all of thirty seconds before he unfastened my pants, shoved his hand in my briefs, and stroked me off. I was in my car, speeding home in a panic, before the cum had dried on my skin.

It got easier after that first time. So easy, in fact, that I spent almost every free moment over the next couple of weeks at that bar playing grab-ass—well, more like grab-dick—with various guys. I wish I could tell you that I was having a ball, swinging from the chandeliers, but the bar had a contemporary décor, so they had recessed lighting. (Okay, give me a minute to laugh at my own joke—I thought that one was pretty funny.)

Ehm, anyway, what I experienced in that bar was

pretty consistent with what I had expected from gay life. There was a lot of drinking, a lot of hooking up, not a lot of talking, and even less of an emotional connection. I was lonely, but, hey, that was nothing new, and at least the sex was good. I would be lying if I said I didn't get off on it, even though it wasn't more than a hand job most nights and a couple of blow jobs from guys who had no compunction about going down on another guy in a public bathroom.

But I would also be lying if I said it was enough. I always knew sex with men would feel good. Hell, all those fantasies had left little doubt in my mind about what got me hot. But I wanted more from life. I wanted someone to come home to at night and to wake up next to in the morning. I wanted someone to laugh with and talk with. I wanted a family.

Knowing I could never have those things with a man was one of the reasons I hated my desires, hated the fact that I couldn't find some way to feel connected on every level with a woman. And the time I spent in that bar didn't do a thing to change any of those feelings. I still wanted men, and as a result, all of the hopes and dreams I'd had for my life seemed so far out of reach that I had almost completely given up on wishing for them.

"BEN? WHAT the hell!"

The guy who was pressed against me was suddenly yanked away, leaving me standing in the corner of the bar with my pants open and my dick hanging out. My hands immediately covered my groin, and I quickly turned to face the wall and put myself away.

"Jesus, Noah! I wasn't completely dressed."

When I turned back around, my brother was looking at me like I was the stupidest person on earth. It wasn't the first time he had graced me with that particular expression, so I recognized it well.

"You did not just complain to me about leaving you exposed. You're in a fucking bar with your cock hanging out, dumb shit!"

Okay, he was right, but I was flustered, and I didn't want to give him the satisfaction of winning yet another argument. "Well, nobody could see that it was hanging out until you pulled...uh, until you pulled...him away."

Noah winced and closed his eyes. Then he took a deep breath. "You didn't even bother asking for a name, did you? Damn it, Ben!"

Before I could formulate a response, Clark walked up and took his customary spot by Noah's side. "Ben, hey! What are you doing here?" He smiled broadly at me.

Noah rolled his eyes. "As far as I can tell, he's doing everything possible to complicate his life."

Clark looked back and forth between us. "Hey, I have an idea," he finally said. "Aaron and Zach were just saying we could go to their place to hang out, since it's so crowded here tonight." He turned to me. "How do you feel about joining us?"

"Uh," I stammered. "I feel like a college girl being asked to go out with Ted Bundy."

The pained expression in Clark's eyes made me stop and shake off my exasperation with my brother. Clark and I had been good friends once, and I was the one responsible for crippling that friendship. Shocker, isn't it? Hey, this whole put-my-foot-in-my-mouth-and-act-like-a-class-A-deranged-lunatic shtick wasn't new. I had been honing that particular skill for years.

"I'd love to come hang out with you guys. Thanks for the invite, Clark." I got a grateful smile from Clark and then turned to my brother. "Noah, that okay with you?"

He nodded briskly. "It's fine. It'll give us time to talk about when you went from being a buttoned-up lawyer to being a complete slut."

CLARK AND Noah had come to that bar with their friends, so they didn't have their car. They insisted on riding with me back to their friends' house, presumably because they figured I would have ditched them otherwise. They were probably right.

Door to door, the trip took no longer than twelve

minutes, but by the time their friend Aaron pulled his front door open, I was already ready to strangle Noah. I mumbled something about being thirsty, stomped into the kitchen, and collapsed onto a chair.

"So, I take it your brother wasn't too happy about finding you making out with that guy at the bar tonight?"

I looked up to identify the person talking. It was my brother's friend Zach. He walked over, pulled up a chair, and sat next to me. Great, now Noah's friends were going to lecture me. I glared at the small guy, hoping he would back off. "Hey, I'm not judging you," he said. "No matter how much fucking around you've been doing, if we compare the number of notches on our bedposts...well, all I'd have left is sawdust."

I was ready to lay into him for making fun of me. I didn't know Zach well, but he was pretty close friends with Clark and Noah, so I had been around him at least a handful of times, and I knew he was in a serious relationship. Whenever I saw him, he was always sitting in Aaron's lap or sucking on his face. And the blond couldn't look at Zach without getting all dreamy-eyed. It was sweet and romantic and it made me want to put my fist through the wall. No way was Zach the hookup type.

"I can see that you don't believe me, but I'm not being an asshole here. I'm not like your brother and Clark. I didn't meet my soul mate in high school and declare my everlasting devotion or some shit. Believe me, I did a lot of playing around and had a lot of fun before I met Aaron and he settled my ass down. Well, not literally, 'cause he gives my ass a solid workout very regularly, but you get the idea."

I started coughing and tried to pretend that something had gone down the wrong pipe. I was pretty sure he didn't fall for it, though, because there hadn't been anything other than my tongue in my mouth. He waggled his eyebrows, and I couldn't help but laugh. The guy was charming, in a really odd sort of way.

"Right. So you played the field and then you met Prince Charming and figured out what real happiness means, right? That's the moral of the story," I said.

Zach got up, walked over to the freezer, and dug out a bottle of vodka. Then he got two glasses out of the cabinet and came back over to sit down next to me.

"Yeah, in a sense. I mean, I'm really happy now. Satisfied deep down, you know? But that doesn't mean I wasn't happy before I met Aaron." He poured two glasses, pushed one over to me, then downed his in one gulp. "I was living in LA. I had a fun job, lots of friends, different guys every night. And the plural isn't an accident." He paused and winked. "I was having a great time and I was happy. Not the same as I am now, but that doesn't mean I wasn't enjoying myself, 'cause I was. I was having fun."

I felt vindicated somehow, even if his description of his life pre-Aaron didn't sound exactly like mine. It actually made me a little uncomfortable, truth be told. Like he was living on a porn set, but maybe he was exaggerating, the way guys sometimes do. Anyway, I felt better. "See, you understand. So why does my brother have to be so uptight and get on my case all the time?"

Even as I said the words, I realized how ridiculous I sounded. Noah wasn't uptight, and I wasn't thirteen years old. So why did I sound like a whiny teenager?

"You want the truth, Ben, or do you want me blow smoke up your ass?" He was serious when he asked the question. Then he blinked and cracked up. "Oh, shit! I've done that before. Not sexy at all." He fake shuddered.

I shuddered for real and hoped he thought I was just kidding around. "About my brother? I want you to tell me the truth."

"I think the reason your brother's giving you shit is because what you were doing at the bar isn't the same as what I did during all those years I was single and living it up."

I didn't think he meant that what I had been doing was way tamer than what he was implying his life had once been. "How do you mean?"

"I mean that I was having a good time. Sure, I was fucking around, but I was happy. And I don't need to know you well to know that one thing you aren't is happy. So I gotta ask myself, what the fuck are you doin'?"

I glared at him, ready to defend myself and tell him off. But I couldn't. He was right. I wasn't happy. I wasn't living it up or whatever he said about his single days. I was miserable.

He nudged his chin toward my glass and refreshed his own drink. I shook my head to let him know I didn't need more, then lifted my glass to my mouth and sipped at the vodka. I was used to beer and wine, not hard liquor, and I didn't really like it.

"Come on, now. It's not that fucking bad. Whatever the hell's eating at you, it's not that bad." He smiled suddenly and shifted in his seat. "Hey, you know what they say you should do when life gives you lemons?"

The sudden change in topic made my head spin. "Make lemonade?" I answered weakly.

"Lemonade? Who the fuck do you hang out with, Girl Scouts? No, when life gives you lemons, you add vodka and make a lemon drop. So here's what's gonna happen. You're gonna chug that drink so I can pour you another one. And when that one's done, we'll repeat the cycle until you're totally wasted. Then we'll pour your drunk ass into the guest room bed, and tomorrow you'll wake up with a nasty as fuck hangover and an empty stomach. Just try to aim for the trash can that I'll leave next to your bed, yeah? I like the sheets in that room. We make use of them every once in a while just to spice things up."

I only realized my mouth was gaping open when he reached over and pushed my chin up.

"Why would I do that? How will getting drunk help anything?" I asked.

Zach smirked. "Oh, it won't help. It's just your farewell pity party. Meaning farewell to your fucking pity. It's your last night feeling sorry for yourself, so live it up. Get plastered, cry about how unjust *it* all is. Not that I know shit about your particular 'it', but whatever's got you all wound up, you can cuss at it and shout at it and whatever the fuck else you wanna do."

He handed me the bottle, got up from the table, and kept talking as he opened the fridge, pulled out some lemons, and started slicing them. "But tomorrow morning, you need to wake up and start taking responsibility for your life. We've all had shit to go through, Ben, some of us worse than others. But wallowing doesn't do dick to get it fixed. Hey, consider yourself lucky, you've got your brother and Clark and Aaron to help you get through it. They're good guys and they care about you. I'm sure they'd be happy to stay up all night talking, if that's what you want."

"What about you? Aren't you going to join the talking extravaganza?"

He turned to me, grinned, and shook his head. "Nah, I'm just the guy who'll hold your hand while you drink yourself into a stupor. Emotions and talking aren't my style."

I thought about arguing with him and telling him he was doing a bang-up job talking to me about my emotions, but I decided to take him up on his offer instead. A good bender and then I would pull my head out of my ass and take control of my life. Because Zach was right, I hadn't been happy over the past couple of weeks, and the bar hookups weren't helping. Frankly, I hadn't been happy in...well... forever.

Except for the time I had spent with Micah. I had been happy then. Really happy.

Okay, bender now, thinking tomorrow. I swallowed down my drink and slammed the empty glass on the table. "I think we're gonna need bigger glasses."

CHAPTER FOURTEEN

"SO LET me ask you guys something," I said, noticing that my tongue felt unusually heavy. Maybe it was time to stop drinking those lemon drops.

"Ask away," Aaron replied with a smile.

"Would you ever be with a guy who wasn't, uh, out?"

I figured there was no harm in talking openly with them. I mean, all four of them were gay men in stable relationships. That was what Micah said he wanted, so maybe they could give me some insight. Clearly, the vodka had unlocked the door in my brain that I had used to section off all thoughts of Micah. It hadn't been working anyway, but sitting in Zach and Aaron's living room, feeling tired, relaxed, and drunk, it was hopeless to try to ignore the ache in my heart. I missed him so much.

"No way," Noah said harshly. "I'd never agree to be some guy's dirty little secret."

Yeah, that wasn't a surprise. My brother was very black and white.

"Come on, Noah," Clark interjected. "What if he had a good reason?"

"I get that people have reasons, angel, sometimes

even good reasons." Noah wrapped his arm around Clark's shoulders as he spoke. It amazed me how my usually gruff brother sounded so gentle when he spoke to his partner. "But unless he was making steps to come out, I don't think I'd want to get involved. I want to be able to celebrate holidays together, go out without looking over our shoulders, be a central part of each other's life. How could I do that if my partner was hiding me?"

When he explained it that way, Noah's issues with our parents suddenly made sense. They had forbidden Noah from bringing Clark into their home, so my brother had stopped coming over. I thought he was doing it to spite them, just his usual stubborn antics. But now I understood. Clark was the center of Noah's world. He wanted his partner with him. Noah had the strength to walk away from anyone who refused to allow him to be himself. I wondered whether I could ever do the same.

"What about you, Aaron?" Clark asked. "Would you date a guy who was still in the closet?"

Aaron chewed on his bottom lip and furrowed his brow, thinking over the question. "I don't know. I mean, it's hard to answer a question like that in the abstract. Who knows how any of us would act if we were really crazy about a guy, right? But I can tell you that one of the things that attracted me to Zach right from the start was how sure and confident he was in himself." He turned to his partner, and his blue eyes sparkled with pride. "I admired his strength and his sense of self. And I think respecting the guy you're with is the key to a relationship. I can't think of anybody I respect more than Zach."

Zach snickered and got up off Aaron's lap, where he had been sitting all night. "All right, big guy. It's time for us to go to bed before everybody goes into a hypoglycemic coma from listening to you gush." He turned to me. "Ben, the invitation to crash here still stands. The guest room is the first one on the right. It has its own bathroom, and there are fresh towels in there. If you hear any screaming or grunting in the middle of the night, that's just Aaron fucking me into the mattress, so don't run into our room in a panic." He hesitated and then spoke again. "Well, I mean, if you want to watch, we keep the door unlocked. It's usually a pretty good show."

Aaron shook his suddenly red face and took Zach's hand, following him to the bedroom. "Good night, guys. Thanks for coming over," he called out over his shoulder. "We'll see you for church on Sunday. Lock up on your way out."

"Since when do you go to church?" I asked.

"By church, he means brunch," Clark responded. "We have a standing date every Sunday with a group of guys. You're welcome to join us anytime." He stood and started picking up empty glasses. "I'm going to wash these out so they don't wake up to a mess in the morning. You guys can finish talking."

When Clark left the room, Noah turned to me. "I'm sorry if I was a little, uh, harsh earlier."

"Saying you were a little harsh is like saying Jeffrey Dahmer had odd eating habits," I mumbled under my breath. Well, I was going for a quiet mumble. All that vodka made volume control a bit of a challenge.

"Damn, Ben, what's with the serial killer references tonight? You're starting to freak me out."

I shrugged and almost fell off the couch.

"You're drunk," Noah observed.

I nodded. "Prolly."

"Well, maybe it's a good time for us to talk."

"Huh?" My brother wasn't making any sense. Or else I wasn't able to comprehend a simple sentence. Either scenario seemed plausible.

"Maybe you won't put up your walls like you usually do and you can just listen to me for once," he explained.

"I always listen to you, Noah."

"No, you don't. But I know it's not all your fault. I don't have to be such an asshole all the time." He ran his fingers through his dark hair. "The reason I gave you a hard time tonight is because you deserve better than bar hookups. That's not who you are."

I rested my head on the back of the couch and closed my eyes. "I'm an idiot," I said. "We could create a new drinking game where everyone takes a shot every time I do something stupid. We'd all spend our life wasted."

"You're not an idiot. A lot of guys I know who came out later, like you, went nuts at first. It was like a second adolescence or something. They'd hit the bars and bathhouses, party too hard, and get lost for a while before they finally got their shit together. That is if they ever got their shit together at all." He paused, and I felt his hand on my shoulder. I opened my eyes and met his concerned gaze. "I don't want that for you, Ben. You're a good brother and a good person. Don't think I don't know that. I'm glad you're in my life."

My jaw dropped. Noah had literally never been that nice to me. Not ever. He continued talking. "So I take it things didn't work out with that guy you were telling me about a couple of months ago. Did he drop you because you're not out? Is that why you were asking those questions earlier?"

"Sort of. He hinted around about meeting Mom and Dad, and I freaked out on him. But I never told him why exactly. I mean, I tried, but it came out all wrong and I just made everything worse. That conversation alone was worthy of a full bottle's worth of shots."

I curled up on the couch and rested my head on my brother's lap. I knew I was acting like a baby, but I didn't care. The ache in my chest had spread to my entire body.

"You want to get him back?" Noah asked quietly.

"More than anything," I answered with a sigh. "But that's not gonna happen. He doesn't want me anymore. I don't blame him, either. I really blew it, Noah."

"Maybe you're right and maybe you're not. There's only one way to find out. If you really want him, then you need to talk to him. You have to be honest, completely honest. Tell him why you freaked about Mom and Dad, tell him you're just now coming out, tell him everything. Then it's up to him to decide if he's willing to give it another go."

I ENDED up sleeping over at Noah and Clark's house. They lived just a couple of streets over from Zach and Aaron, so we left a note thanking those guys for their hospitality and ambled home. Well, for me it was more like stumbled, but I got there without falling on my ass. Is that applause I hear? Thanks.

Noah's guest room had shutters that did a nice job of keeping the sun out, which was great because I was able to sleep in. By the time my body finally felt ready to face the world, it was after ten. I lay in the bed and stared at the ceiling for a while, thinking about what I needed to do.

I could go to Micah's house and beg him to take me back, but that wouldn't work. First off, he probably wasn't there. Even though it was Saturday, I guessed Micah was at the office. His big trial was coming up, and everyone on his team was working themselves ragged around the clock. But that wasn't the only problem. Convincing the man I so desperately wanted to give me another chance wouldn't accomplish anything if I just turned right around and blew it again. So before I tried to get him back, I had to make some changes in my life.

With that decision made, I threw off the blanket and dragged my ass into the bathroom. I brushed my teeth with the new toothbrush Clark had left for me on the bathroom counter. Then I flossed and made a rookie too-hung-over-to-think-clearly error. Don't rub your eyes right after manipulating minty floss. The experience is way too refreshing.

After my shower I felt almost human. I got dressed and walked into the kitchen, pausing at the doorway. Noah and Clark were standing close together. Clark's arms were resting on Noah's shoulders. Noah had one hand on Clark's neck and the other on his lower back. And they were talking quietly to each other, affection clear in their expressions and tone. I wanted that kind of connection so much it made my teeth hurt.

I remembered what Micah said to me the last time we talked. (Yeah, I was describing it as a "talk." Don't laugh at me. I'd had a rough night, okay?) Anyway, he said he didn't want a fuck buddy. Was that what he thought I wanted? Well, I couldn't blame him. I had spent so long thinking that was all there was to being gay that I hadn't conceived of a lasting relationship with another man. Maybe that belief had come through in my behavior, both with Micah and over the past couple of weeks of bar hopping and hookups.

My brother had tried explaining it to me more than once. Hell, he had been modeling it for me. But I still never understood that it could be true, that it could be real, and that I could experience it. As I stood in Noah's kitchen, watching the emotions that were clear in every glance and every touch he shared with Clark, I realized with an almost painful clarity that it was possible for a man to truly be in love with another man.

Living three decades without having experienced that emotion or thinking I ever could, I had taken longer than I should have to recognize it. But suddenly, I realized that I did understand what it meant to love someone. There was no other word to describe the joy that surged through me when Micah smiled in my direction, the way my heart raced when he touched me, and the way my stomach had hurt since I had let him slip through my fingers. Oh, God. I didn't want to lose him.

"Morning, rock star," Clark laughed, pulling me out of my thoughts.

"What?" I glared at him.

He shook his head and walked over the fridge. "Nothing, man. Just thinking about last night. I don't think I've seen you that drunk since pledge week."

I sank into a chair at their kitchen table. "Yeah? Well, nineteen-year-old frat boys have nothing on your friend Zach. Something tells me he could charm a nun into sinning."

"Oh, he's got no interest in nuns. Now a priest..." Clark

shrugged. Then he set a bottle of Gatorade and a vitamin in front of me.

"What's this?" I asked.

"Hangover helper: B12 and Gatorade."

I popped the vitamin into my mouth and swallowed it down with the sports drink. "This really works?"

Clark nodded and then went back to the fridge, pulling out eggs and other breakfast ingredients.

Noah flipped a chair around and straddled it, resting his arms on the back and looking at me intently. "Actually, you don't look bad at all. Your eyes are a little bloodshot, but otherwise you're just as gorgeous as ever."

"Gorgeous enough to face the parental units?" I fiddled with the label on the bottle as I asked the question.

My brother chuckled. "They've seen me in much worse condition. But if you're not up for it, just ditch them and blame me. Tell them I needed you for something, or whatever."

It was amazing how good that simple comment made me feel. Knowing my brother had my back. "Why are you being so nice to me all of a sudden?" I asked.

"Because I meant what I said last night." He rested a big hand on my shoulder and squeezed it. "You're a good brother."

I nodded and swallowed down the lump in my throat. I had tried so hard for so long to keep our family together. It hadn't been easy with Noah. He had always been pissed off at all of us. And I had made my share of mistakes along the way; some of them should have been unforgivable. But there I was, sitting in Noah's kitchen on a Saturday morning, talking with him and watching Clark make breakfast. Nobody was yelling or hitting or slamming doors. Whatever else happened later that day, I had family to fall back on.

"Thanks, but I need to go talk to them. I need to tell them the truth." I paused and gathered my courage, willing myself to say the words without sounding ashamed. "They need to know that both of their sons are gay."

CHAPTER FIFTEEN

MY MOTHER was crying and my father was pacing, but I hadn't completely fallen apart. All right, so I hadn't hit it out of the park with my big announcement, but it was an improvement over how I had expected things to go. I won't say it wasn't terrifying—my trembling hands and nausea would show me as a liar. But I had done it. I had walked into my parents' colonial style house, sat down on the antique Chippendale wing chair in their perfectly decorated living room, and calmly told them I was gay.

You heard me right, folks. I, Benjamin Isaac Forman, had come out of the closet. Scary, yes. But also freeing.

"You're not *that way*, Benjamin," my father shouted as he stormed back and forth in front of me, somehow managing to avoid knocking over any of the Lladró collectibles. "You're an athlete, for goodness sake! Just look at you—you're a man. Why would you say these vile things about yourself?"

Hearing my father talk left no doubt in my mind about where the insidious little voice that had been haunting me for years had been getting his script. Well, I was done acknowledging that voice. I knew he would probably keep infiltrating my brain, but that didn't mean I had to listen.

"Being an athlete has nothing to do with it. I would think Noah had already proven that one to you. And, yes, I am a man. A gay man." It was a little less difficult every time I said the words. "Why can't you just accept that and move on? Why do you need to take cuts at me and tear me down?"

"We're not tearing you down, son," my mother said with a shaky voice, a damp tissue dabbing at the sides of her eyes. At least she was no longer bawling. "We know you love your brother. We love him too. But Noah has always done everything he could think of under the sun to rebel. There is absolutely no reason for you to follow his lifestyle choices."

Great. When Noah came out, it was my fault for introducing him to Clark. Now it was Noah's fault for introducing me to...lifestyle choices? What the hell did that even mean? I had thought it myself, even said it—a gay lifestyle. But it made no sense.

"A lifestyle choice is being a Republican or a Protestant, Mom. Being gay isn't a lifestyle and it isn't a choice. It's who I am."

See that? I put together an articulate sentence. I promise you, I was an actual lawyer and I talked to people for a living. I know my behavior so far has made you wonder, but hopefully I'm redeeming myself.

"It doesn't have to be who you are." My father sat down next to me. "There are people you can talk to. Let us help you, Ben. We're your parents and we love you."

I shook my head. There was nothing anybody could

say that would change how I felt when I looked at Micah. I wanted what Noah and Clark had—that heart-slamming, stomach-dropping, dick-hardening excitement I had only ever experienced with another man—and the freedom to enjoy it.

It would disappoint my parents. It wasn't what they wanted for me. But I couldn't continue going through life only partially engaged, constantly hiding, and always afraid someone would figure out the truth. Because the fact was if I didn't take a stand and start living the life I had been given, I wouldn't be *living* at all. It had taken me thirty-one years to figure that out, but I had finally gotten there, and I wasn't going to let my parents push me backward.

"You love the son you want me to be," I said. "As for who I actually am...well, you don't really know me. How can you love someone you don't know?"

I listened to my own words and came to a startling realization. My parents weren't the only people who didn't know me. I had been hiding for so long that I wasn't even sure I knew myself. And how could *I* love someone I didn't know?"

I KNEW that I should just go home and get myself together. I had been up late the night before, I was still a little hungover, and I had just barely survived the most emotional conversation

I had ever had with my parents. I wasn't at my best, either emotionally or physically. But when I left my parents' house, I didn't drive home. I got onto the highway and drove to EC West. And I wasn't going to my brother's place.

It was after six by the time I got to Micah's house, and it was Saturday. I hoped that meant he would be at home and not at the office. With a million different thoughts skittering through my mind and no clue what I planned to say, I walked up his paved sidewalk and rang his doorbell.

The door swung open, and I found myself face-to-face with a gorgeous guy. He was wearing cotton shorts and a T-shirt with the sleeves ripped off, so it was impossible for me to miss his bulging muscles.

"Oh! I, uh, I was looking for Micah," I stammered.

He smiled and waved me in. "You're Noah Forman's brother, right? Ben, is it?" He held his hand out.

I nodded and shook his hand. "Yes."

"I'm David Miller. We've met a time or two. I think the last time was at Noah and Clark's barbeque earlier this spring."

Once I looked at his face and made my brain focus, I recognized him. He had just been out of context at Micah's house. Wait. Why was he at Micah's house?

"It's nice to see you again, David. Is, um, is Micah…"

"Micah's in his bedroom getting dressed."

I gasped involuntarily and started backing up toward the door. Walking in on Micah and another guy right after they'd... I had to get the hell out of there.

I should have known Micah would have moved on. Someone as wonderful as him probably had a couple of guys on deck or wouldn't have had any trouble meeting a new guy. And from the look of things, he had sure as hell upgraded from me. David was drop-dead gorgeous and, based on my memory of past interactions with him, really nice.

David's tricep bulged as his arm flew out and he grabbed me by the shoulder. "Wait," he said. "I was just leaving. You stay."

Before I could argue with him, he was out the door and I was standing alone in Micah's entryway.

"All right, David. I've got a lot of tension to work off, so I hope you have time for a long..." Micah's voice tapered off when he saw me. He halted to a sudden stop several feet away. "Ben."

I couldn't quite tell if he sounded happy or frightened when he said my name. Whatever the case, he was within arm's reach before I realized I had been moving. I couldn't help myself. I was so tired, so scared about everything going on in my life, so lonely without him. And he was right there. I had to get closer.

"Where's David?" he asked.

I shook my head to clear my thoughts and answered. "I'm sorry. I think it was my fault. He said he was just leaving, but he probably didn't realize that you weren't done, uh"—I blinked back tears—"working off your tension."

And just like that, I was pulled into Micah's arms. He held me close, rubbed my back with one hand, and stroked my hair with the other. His gravelly voice was soothing in my ear. "Shhh, honey. We were just going to the gym. Other than my own hand, that's the only kind of tension release I've had since you. David's got a partner and a son at home. There's nothing going on between us."

Big hands cupped my cheeks and tilted my head back up so our eyes met. Thumbs swiped under my eyes, wiping away tears I couldn't stop from falling. And then those strong arms pulled me close again.

I pressed my face into his neck and closed my eyes. God, I'd missed how good he smelled, how wonderful it felt to be held, the taste of his skin. I thought about the last one when my tongue reached out and took a lick.

"Talk to me, Ben. You're trembling and crying. This can't all be about David."

I shook my head and raised it until our lips met. He opened for me right away, tilting his head and sucking my tongue into his mouth. Our bodies lined up perfectly, just like they always had, and I dragged my erection against his.

"It's not all about David," I whispered when we finally broke for air. "But can we talk later? I just need to feel you right now." I desperately hoped he wouldn't turn me away. "Please, Micah," I pleaded.

He nodded and leaned in for another kiss. My hands took hold of his T-shirt, pushing it up his chest and exposing smooth, hot skin. I mapped his body with my hands, feeling the anxious ball that had been living in my stomach for two weeks start to dissolve as those familiar long, sleek muscles tightened under my touch.

He shoved his hands between us and pulled my polo shirt out of my pants, yanking it up and over my head. Then he stripped off his T-shirt and came back for more kisses. Lips, tongues, and even teeth got in on the act. Micah's fingers dug into my hips and pulled me forward. Then he rolled his hips and thrust his hard cock against mine.

"Bed," he practically growled as he dragged his teeth over the soft skin under my ear and worked his way to my shoulder.

"Too far," I answered and then pulled him to the sofa.

"Yeah, okay."

Micah's eyes were unfocused, his pupils wide and his skin flushed. I loved seeing him so turned on, and knowing I did that to him made me lose whatever rein I'd had on my control. He unbuttoned my pants as I toed off my shoes, and then I pushed my briefs down and stood naked in front of him.

He crowded me toward the couch, not letting our lips separate for more than a second at a time. I fell backward onto the soft cushions and watched him hook his thumbs into the sides of his shorts before shoving them down along with his jock and then straddling my lap. One of his hands cupped the back of my head, pulling my mouth toward his, and his other hand reached between us and circled our erections.

"Yes! Micah, yes!" I moaned and arched my back, raising my hips off the couch and pushing my cock into his hand.

"Missed this," he whispered into my neck. "Missed you."

After that, we were done talking. Our mouths fused together, our hips rolled, and we thrust in tandem, racing toward our quickly approaching orgasms. I got there first and cried out his name as I coated his hand with wet heat. He rubbed my seed onto his dick and gave himself another couple of strokes before his head flew back and his eyes closed.

"Ben!" His body shook as his cock pulsed thick, white release all over his stomach and chest. Then he collapsed against me and dropped his forehead onto my shoulder. "Damn, it's good between us. So fucking good." His voice was rough and sexy as hell.

"For me too," I said softly and massaged his scalp. "What do I need to do to keep this, Micah, to keep you? What do you want?"

He raised his head and blue eyes locked with mine. His tongue came out and licked his swollen lips, and he furrowed his brow in thought. "Everything. I want everything. But only if that's what you want to give. I'm not gonna keep chasing you, Ben. I want you, but you have to want me too."

A nervous laugh escaped, and I found myself snorting

it back. Yeah, not a sexy move, but it made Micah smile. "I do want you. I want you more than anything or anyone I've ever wanted in my life. I promise that I'm done running away from you. If you really want everything, I'm all in."

"All in, huh?" Twinkling eyes gazed at me with fondness. "No more acting like it's just about sex or it's completely casual between us? No more running away?" I nodded, and he arched one eyebrow. "Should I take a chance and ask what brought on this change?"

Was there any way to cling to a man without being clingy? Because I held onto Micah so tight in that moment I was worried he would think I was a freak and retract his invitation for everything. But verbal contracts were enforceable, we'd had a meeting of the minds, and I had accepted his offer, so that was binding as far as I was concerned. I wondered whether a good blow job would be considered acceptable compensation or whether it would make the contract voidable as against public policy.

Dear God, this wasn't the bar exam. Time to get my head back into the game.

"You think maybe we can take a shower before I answer that question? It's not so simple, and I'm in that stage where sticky is turning into itchy," I responded.

As if my words made him realize he had the same problem, Micah started scratching at the drying cum on his stomach. "Yeah, okay. Good plan." He climbed off my lap and pulled me to my feet. "We can conserve water and shower together. I'll even wash your back."

MICAH KNEELED on his bathmat, nuzzling and licking my balls as he tenderly dried my legs. My growling stomach interrupted the festivities.

Micah kissed my belly and laughed. "All right, all right. I can take a hint." He got to his feet and quickly dried the rest of my body. "Come on, I'll feed you."

I kissed his cheek and pulled him in for a quick hug. "Thank you."

We hung our towels and walked out of his bathroom into the bedroom. Micah immediately headed for the door, but then he stopped and turned around. "Sorry, forgot about pants. Hold on, I'll get a pair of sweats or something for both of us."

"No, don't," I snapped, sounding much harsher than I intended. "I mean, I like seeing you naked, and it's just us here, so there's no reason to get dressed."

He tilted his head to the side and appraised me carefully, as though he could somehow figure me out just from the surface. Clearly he didn't realize my many layers of fucked-upness couldn't be deciphered with mere human eyes. Even X-ray vision wouldn't have done the job.

Eventually, his gaze softened, and he walked over to me, grasping my hip with one hand and the nape of my neck with the other and pulling me tightly against him. "It's always been just us here, honey, and you've never been comfortable being naked outside of this room unless we were fooling around." He leaned his forehead against mine. "I'm not out to change you, Ben. I like you just the way you are." A short pause, and then, "Well, just the way you are without the temper and the pushing me away. But we've already covered that. Please don't feel like you need to do something that makes you uncomfortable for my sake."

He was so wonderful, and I knew I didn't deserve him. But he seemed to want me, and I sure wasn't going to point out that he was settling for less than he could get. No, I was going to hold on tight and fight like hell to keep him. Hey, I may show up a little late to the party, but once I get there, I've got the lampshade on my head and I'm dancin' on the table.

"I guess I'm a bit uncomfortable, but I'm not doing it for your sake. I'm doing it for mine. I really do love looking at your body, and I'm done letting the voices in my head keep me from living my life."

Oh, shit! Did I just tell him I heard voices? Dear God, I sounded like a total freak show. I mean, I *was* a total freak show, but that was something I tried to keep under wraps.

"Man, the voices in your head sound pretty harsh." He slapped my ass and then took my hand and pulled me toward the door. "No matter how perverted my thoughts get, the voices in my head tell me I'm perfectly normal."

I laughed in relief. Yeah, I was keeping him, even if it meant that I hard to play hardball with those damn internal voices. I wasn't going to drive away a man who understood me even when I didn't understand myself, a man who made me feel safe and happy, a man I loved.

CHAPTER SIXTEEN

"ALL RIGHT, here we are," Micah said as he pulled yet another container out of the microwave and set it in front of me. "It's like a pupu platter of leftovers. With all of these bits and pieces, we should have enough food to fill us up."

I spooned a couple of bites of lasagna, a little enchilada, and some General Tso's chicken onto my plate. "Tomorrow we're going to the grocery store. Between the two of us, we should be able to put together a meal or two. Maybe grilled chicken or hamburgers or something."

Micah beamed. "Sounds good. It seems like too much effort to cook when it's just for me, but if it's for both of us..." He let his voice trail off and then took my free hand and squeezed it. "Are you ready to talk about earlier tonight?"

No, I wasn't ready. I wanted Micah to think I was strong and confident and not an emotional wreck. But I was done hiding, and I wasn't going to lie to him. Well, not anymore—I wasn't going to lie to him *anymore*.

"I haven't been completely honest with you," I started slowly and looked at his face to gauge his reaction. True to form, he kept his expression unchanged. Damn, that man would be an asset in a high-pressure cross-examination.

"The reason I got so angry when we were talking about you coming with me to my parents' house is because they didn't know about me, and I was scared they'd figure it out." Okay, yeah, that made no sense whatsoever. I took a drink of water and tried again. "What I mean is, I wasn't out. I told them that I'm gay today for the first time."

The surprise and confusion in Micah's eyes told me he hadn't been expecting to hear that particular confession. Before he could say anything, I kept talking, needing to get it all out there. "Don't get me wrong, they're not bad people. It's just that they have certain beliefs and being gay doesn't mesh with them."

Micah nodded and took a bite of some sort of leftover beef dish. Well, I supposed he was giving me room to talk, so I did. I talked and Micah listened.

I told him about my childhood. "It was idyllic in a lot of ways—upper middle class upbringing, stay-at-home mom driving me to activities and leagues, a dad who played catch with me in the backyard, and a younger brother I loved. But in other ways, growing up was...numbing.

"I knew I was different from a really young age, and I always knew it was wrong. I don't want you to think that my parents are like awful, hateful people or anything, because they're really not. But their negative opinions about gay people were very clear from the things they said and the way they acted. And I was constantly afraid they'd figure out that I was one of *those people*. For a couple of years right after puberty hit, I even stopped having friends over because I was worried my parents would notice how I looked at other guys. It was exhausting, and I wanted so much to just be normal."

I told him about my dating history. "I thought maybe if I ignored it or went out with girls, it'd just it'd go away. All that practice hiding in front of my family taught me some useful skills. Like if you smile a lot and make jokes, and if you're good at sports and dress a certain way, people want to be around you. So I never had any problem making friends, never got into any trouble, never had trouble finding girls to date. My parents were happy, they were proud of me. And I was...well, I was getting by, I guess."

And then we were done eating, the leftover containers were in the trash, the dishes were in the dishwasher, and we were on our way back to the bedroom. We crawled into bed and lay on our sides facing each other. Micah traced my ear, the curve of my cheek, and my jawline with his finger. "I owe you an apology, Ben," he said tenderly. "I'm sorry."

I sat up in surprise. "What do you mean?"

"I just assumed you were out. I should have realized you weren't from some of the things you said and did. But I knew your brother before I'd ever met you, and Noah is just really, um, in your face, you know? About everything. I guess it never occurred to me that his brother would be—"

"A spineless wimp cowering in the closet," I finished the sentence for him and slid onto my back, squeezing my eyes shut.

The mattress shifted and then Micah's body moved over mine until he was straddling me with his knees on either side of my hips and his elbows next to my shoulders.

"No, honey. I don't think you're spineless. And I don't think you're a wimp." He kissed my forehead, and I opened my eyes. "I get it, Ben," he said. "I know what it's like to deny it, to fight it, to try to change it. And I remember how scary it is when none of those things work and you finally have to admit to yourself that you like guys, that you're gay and that you're always going to be."

"So what did you do?" I asked in a whisper. "How did you deal with it?"

He paused and dropped a kiss on my lips. "I realized that when I go to sleep at night, I'm the only one inside my head, so at the end of the day, I had to find a way to make myself someone I could stand or, in a perfect world, someone I could like. So I did the only thing I could do—I accepted it. It's amazing how just that one thing is enough to make it a little better."

I nodded because I understood. As emotionally draining and painful as the past twenty-four hours had been, there was also a big part of me that felt lighter somehow. Like just the act of telling my parents the truth had dissolved a heavy weight I had been carrying. "And then?" I asked.

"Well, then you just...you just live." He stretched out until his legs were tangled with mine, our chests were pressed together, and our eyes lined up. "To paraphrase from one of my favorite musicals, 'There are days when you'll be faced with a whole lotta ugly from a never-ending parade of stupid.' So it's not always easy, but that's life, right? You might lose some friends along the way, but you'll also gain new ones. You might feel uncomfortable in certain places, but you'll become part of a community with other people like us. And whatever happens, you'll be you, the real you. And that right there is worth the price of admission."

"That's some pretty Zen talk for a bulldog litigator," I teased.

"Well, we don't want to let opposing counsel know that. Gotta keep them on their toes, so the whole Zen thing will be our little secret," he said before leaning down and kissing me. Our tongues danced, our hips ground together, and our hands wandered. It felt amazing. "Hey, Ben," Micah asked as he pulled back from yet another in a long lineup of breath-stealing kisses.

"Mmm-hmm," I replied.

"Can I ask you something without you getting upset?" The way his nose was burrowing into my neck made it impossible for me to refuse.

"You can ask me anything. I'm an open book now. You just need to be careful about reading me at bedtime, because I have some pretty scary chapters."

He chuckled softly and squeezed me tight. "When you said that you just came out today, what does that mean, exactly? I gather that you weren't out to your family and that you weren't out at work. But does that mean there haven't been other guys except for me?"

I couldn't stop the blush from spreading up my neck and over my cheeks, but it was a fair question, and I forced myself to answer it without getting defensive. "You're the first guy I've ever been with. I, uh, fooled around a little after we broke up, but it wasn't anything serious."

He dipped his head and kissed me lightly. Then he peppered kisses along my jaw and sucked on my ear lobe. "Is that why you haven't wanted to top me?" His voice was even deeper than usual, the roughness more pronounced. "I've been wondering why you always took things in a different direction when that came up."

"I wanted to, I just…" I tried not to feel embarrassed. I'd had his dick in my body, for Christ's sake. A little conversation shouldn't be an issue. "I wasn't exactly sure what to do, and I was worried that I'd do it wrong or hurt you or something. And it felt really good the other way too, so…" I shrugged and let the thought trail off.

"You know, one of the great things about being gay is that we get to have a lot of flexibility in our sex lives. I know there are guys who like to take only one role in bed, but I've always thought that was kind of a waste. Giving feels great, but so does receiving. At least to me." He reached between us and stroked my dick. "You wanna try doing me tonight to see if you agree?"

I nodded so fast it was a wonder I didn't get whiplash. Micah chuckled once again. Then he leaned down and gnawed on my neck, making his way down my sternum and over to my right nipple. He licked around the brown disk before taking it into his mouth and sucking. I arched up and moaned. Then he gave my right nipple the same treatment before moving down my belly until my hard, leaking cock nudged his chin.

He circled his tongue around my glans, licked up and down my hard length, and then sucked me into his mouth. His right hand wrapped around the base of my dick and held me steady while his mouth worked me over. That wet heat moved up and down, taking me farther and farther into this mouth until I could feel my crown pressing against the back of his throat.

"Micah! Oh, damn, Micah, you gotta stop." Unable to control my own body, I arched my back and pushed myself deeper into his mouth. "I'm not gonna be able to hold back... Micah!"

He came off my dick with a pop and gave me a proud, satisfied look as he leaned over and pulled the bottle of lube and a condom out of the nightstand. I leaned my head back on the pillow and closed my eyes, trying to calm my breathing and push back my impending orgasm. I had actually made some progress when I felt the cool condom on the head of my cock and Micah's hot hand rolling it down. He followed that up with a drizzle of lube and few firm strokes to get me covered, and I had to bite my lip and think of baseball statistics in order to stop myself from exploding right then and there.

Micah's hand disappeared, and then I heard a quiet moan. My eyes popped open, and I almost swallowed my tongue in reaction to the sight that greeted me. Micah was kneeling above me, his head tilted back, eyes closed, brow furrowed in concentration. And his hand was snaked behind his back and moving in a way that left no question as to what he was doing back there.

I tightened my abs and raised myself to a sitting position as I clasped his wrist. "Stop. I wanna do that. Can I?"

His eyelids fluttered open, and he dropped his forehead against mine. "God, yes. How do you want me, honey?"

I wiggled out from underneath him, crawled behind him, and flattened my hand between his shoulder blades, encouraging him down onto his hands and knees. Micah followed my direction without any resistance, getting onto all fours and then spreading his legs a little more and tilting his ass up in invitation. Damn, was that ever sexy.

I moaned his name and reached for the lube, coating my fingers and then circling his pucker with a gentle touch.

"Feels good," he sighed.

"I'm going to push in a finger now."

I gave him a couple of seconds to object, but when he didn't, I slowly pressed my finger into his warm channel.

Micah moaned and rocked backward, taking me all the way down to the knuckle. It was incredible to know that I was making him feel so good, and my confidence rose. One finger became two, two became three, and before I knew it, I was holding Micah's hip steady with one hand and leading my cock to its target with the other.

A slow, steady push got me balls deep inside my lover. I held still, draping my chest over his back and trying to regain a bit of control.

"Still good?" I asked him.

"God, yes. You feel amazing inside me." He moved his hips back and forth, inspiring me to move with him and drag my cock out of his channel until the swollen glans was holding his tight ring open. Then I pushed back in one fast stroke. "Yes!" he shouted. "So good, honey. So damn good."

It was good. More than good. His tight heat surrounding me, welcoming me home, damn near took my breath away. I flattened my hands on the mattress on either side of him, rested my forehead between his shoulder blades, and began moving in earnest.

I thrust my cock in and out of his passage, changing my angle until I hit that spot inside him that made him cry out. And then we moved together, our pace increasing until I could hear the sound of our skin slapping together.

"Aww, fuck, I wanna come," he groaned. "Touch me, honey. God, please touch me."

My right hand moved off the bed and gripped his

cock. It didn't take more than a few firm strokes before he was shouting my name and shooting onto the mattress. His ass clenched around my dick and pulled my orgasm from me.

"Micah, *Micah*!" I chanted his name. "I'm right there. Oh God. Oh God. Yes!"

My entire body shook with the force of my climax. My rhythm disappeared as I pounded into him a few more times and then held myself still deep inside him and filled the condom.

We stayed like that for a while as our pulses slowed. Eventually, I slipped out of his body, tied off the condom, and tossed it into the trash can. Micah flipped onto his back and pulled me down on top of him, holding me close and kissing my neck.

I felt so carefree and happy. It was amazing, really, considering how long I had been certain that my whole world would crumble if I ever let myself act on my feelings for other men. But there I was, in bed with a man, out to my parents, and ready to stop hiding from everyone else. And my world had never felt more right.

"You know, I thought of something else that's good about coming out," Micah's husky voice mumbled into my ear between kisses.

"What's that?" I asked breathlessly.

"Well, sometimes, you're lucky enough to find a guy who can share that new life with you. Someone to laugh with you during the happy times and help prop you up during the hard ones." He lowered his voice, sounding bashful for the first time since I had known him. "Someone you love, who loves you back."

His gaze was piercing, and I heard the question without him saying the words. "Micah?"

"Yeah."

My heart slammed against my ribs, but I gathered my courage and said what I was feeling. "I love you."

The smile that took over his face made every ounce of nerves worthwhile, and I felt like I was batting a thousand when he responded. "I love you too, Ben."

CHAPTER SEVENTEEN

WHEN CONSCIOUSNESS started seeping in the next morning, I realized something was different, but I couldn't place it. Then Micah stirred behind me and what I was feeling became clear—I was happy.

I had been plagued with some version of anxiety-induced stomach pain for so long that I had forgotten it wasn't a normal state of being. But now it was gone. And I had slept the whole night through, no tossing and turning, no waking up and forcing myself to close my eyes and try to get a few more hours in, no recording of my failures playing on a loop in my mind. Damn, I felt good.

"Morning, honey." Micah's morning voice was even rougher than his regular speaking voice. Such a turn-on.

Warm lips pressed gently against the back of my neck, and a warm hand caressed my hip, my waist, and then slid across my ribcage and rubbed lazy circles on my belly. I wiggled back until Micah's hard cock was firmly wedged between my cheeks and then covered his hand with mine, following his slow petting motion. "Good morning. I like waking up like this. It was one of the things I missed most when we were apart."

"Me too," he whispered. "How're you doing? Yesterday was a big day for you."

I shrugged. "I feel really good, the best I've felt in a long time. I know I should be freaking out or something, but I'm really not. I'm just relieved."

I felt Micah nod. "Maybe that's your body's way of telling you it was time."

"Again with the Zen," I laughed. "But yeah, it was time." Micah nibbled on my shoulder, and I kept talking. I really enjoyed being able to share my thoughts so openly, and I knew Micah would be a smart, thoughtful sounding board. "I'm still not sure how to handle things at work. My family is most important, and that's out of the way. Telling my friends will be awkward, but honestly, I haven't been really close with anyone since I screwed things up with Clark, and we seem to be on the mend now. So whatever happens with my other friends, I'll be okay with it. But work…"

Micah kissed the back of my neck again, and his hand brushed over my chest, taking extra time with my nipples. My hand was still on top of his, so I started leading his movements, pushing him lower. I could feel the erection pressed against my backside growing.

"I'll support whatever decision you make." His fingertips made contact with my cock, and his voice got huskier. "I know that doesn't solve the problem, but I just want you to know that my feelings for you aren't contingent on what you do or don't say at the office."

He was right; knowing he would stand by me didn't solve my dilemma over what to do. But it did make me feel better. I turned my head and gave him a gentle kiss. "Thank you."

He nibbled on my lower lip and wrapped his big hand around my cock. As he stroked me, he pushed his dick up and down through the cleft of my ass. I thought about asking him to fuck me, but I didn't want to lose his body heat when he fumbled for a condom, so I enjoyed the feeling of his body so close to mine, his hand steadily heightening my arousal, and his hot breath against my neck and back.

"Feel good, honey?" he asked.

"Uh-huh. Really good," I replied.

"That's all I want, Ben. Just want to make you feel good."

His grip tightened, his pace got faster, and suddenly I was at the edge of a climax. "Ungh, Micah! So close, just a little harder." He gave me what I needed, increasing the speed of his strokes and, with it, the speed of his thrusts against my ass.

I heard him pant, felt his forehead drop between my shoulder blades, and then he gave a couple of hard, desperate pushes. "Right there, honey, I'm right there."

That rough, husky voice, that firm grip combined with smooth strokes and the feeling of Micah's release splashing against my ass and lower back as he called out my name all joined to draw out my orgasm.

"Oh, yes! So good, Micah," I moaned as my dick pulsed and coated Micah's hand with my seed.

He wiped my cum on the sheet and then flattened his hand on my chest and squeezed me tightly. We lay together quietly as our pulses slowed to a normal rate.

"Micah?"

"Uh-huh."

"What's your position on condoms?"

He chuckled. "My position?"

I threw my elbow back into his ribs. Not hard enough to hurt, but enough to startle him.

"Ooomph! All right, all right. I'm sorry for being a smartass. My position on condoms...umm, other than a couple of stupid alcohol-induced mistakes in my early twenties, I've always used them. Safety first and all that."

I nodded. It was the answer I had expected. He had always used a condom when we'd had sex. It was clearly a given to him.

"But," Micah continued in a quieter voice, "I've never been in a really serious relationship, never been in love with the guy I was sleeping with, so if you want us to stop using raincoats, I'm fine with it. As long as we're both clean and we agree that there are no other guys."

I thought about it for a few seconds and then nodded. "I'm not interested in being with other guys. And I'm sure that I'm clean, but I'll go get tested this week, just to confirm."

Before we could talk about it further, I heard my

phone ringing. "That's Noah's ringtone. Mind if I get it?"

Micah patted my belly and then sat up. "Go ahead. I'll go start the shower, and you can join me when you're done talking to your brother."

By the time I got out of bed and got my phone out of my pants pocket, I had missed Noah's call. I dialed him back.

"So you're still alive?" he said.

"Hello and good morning to you too, Noah. And yes, I'm still alive. Why wouldn't I be?"

"Because you walked into the eye of the storm yesterday. Dad called me after you left their house. I didn't answer, but he left a message, which I promptly deleted without listening to most of it. But I got far enough to know that you went through with telling them and that he was his usual hateful self. When I didn't hear from you all night, I was worried you'd gone home and started an excavation into the furthest recesses of your closet. I was giving you another twelve hours and then I was going to send Zach in with more medicine."

"Medicine?" I asked, ignoring his comments about our parents. Noah and the rest of the family had been like oil and water for so long that I had learned to pick my battles with him, knowing the alternative was being written out of his life entirely.

"Yeah, you know, the kind that starts with an 'a' and ultimately ends with you taking a nice relaxing vacation to Betty Ford or becoming intimately familiar with the porcelain god. The magic elixir that finally accomplished what I haven't been able to do in almost a year of nagging—it dragged you out of the closet. Not that I'm supporting turning you into a drunk, but if it gets the job done..."

"It wasn't the alcohol. It was the conversation. It was knowing you're there for me. It was Micah. It was a lot of things, I guess."

"Micah? As in Micah Trains?"

I nodded reflexively and then realized he couldn't see me. "Uh-huh."

"Is he who you were seeing? The guy you're all into but you said wouldn't want anything to do with you because you acted like an ass?"

I suddenly realized that I had never mentioned Micah by name. "Yeah, that's him. But we worked things out, and everything's good." I thought about how understanding Micah had been the previous evening, about how he listened to me talk about my family, the mistakes I had made with Clark and Noah, my insecurities. And I thought about how he hadn't judged me or looked down on me, about how he held me and told me that he loved me. I couldn't keep the grin off my face. "Better than good."

"He's a good choice for you, Ben. I like him. He's smart, he's decent, and I don't think he's the type to dick you around."

I didn't need my brother's approval—his opinion wouldn't have kept me from being with Micah—but I was still grateful for his support. "Thanks, Noah."

"Hey, it's no sweat off my balls. So what are you guys doing today? You want to join us for brunch?"

"Is it just you and Clark, or did I hear Zach and Aaron say something about having brunch with you today?" I asked.

"Yeah, Zach and Aaron will be there. And some of our other friends too. It's a weekly thing. Everyone who's available comes. We eat, drink some mimosas, catch up. I think you've probably met most of the guys at some point, but it'll give you a chance to get to know them better. And I think Micah knows most of them too."

Never did I imagine that my brother would think of me as a friend. But there he was, inviting me to join him for brunch, wanting me to get to know his friends, including me in his life. Yeah, maybe things were going to be tense with my parents for a little while, but finally being honest about who I was had had some positive impacts on my family too. My brother, who'd all but hated us for over fifteen years, was welcoming me into his life. And once I got things worked out with my parents, maybe I would be able to get us all in a room without anybody yelling or storming out. Hey, it's good to have goals, right? Why not swing for the fences?

"Micah's in the shower, but I'll ask him and call you back. He might have to work today. His trial prep is really heating up now."

"Sounds good. Even if he's working, you should still join us. It'll be fun. We're meeting at Roxy's Diner at eleven."

AFTER A long shower that involved a surprising amount of conversation and, less surprisingly, some fun groping, Micah and I went into the bedroom to get dressed. I was shaking out my polo shirt, hoping I could somehow keep it from looking like it had been balled up on the floor for half a day, when Micah walked over.

"Here, try this on." He held a T-shirt out to me. "It should fit you."

I took the shirt and slipped it on. "Thanks. My pants are fine, so if you loan me a pair of socks, I'll be all set."

He dug through his drawer and handed me a pair of white socks. I skipped the briefs and pulled my pants on.

Micah groaned and reached over to me, cupping my dick and balls through my pants and giving them a squeeze. "Knowing you're free-balling is going to make it hard to concentrate on anything else during brunch."

I waggled my eyebrows and smirked as I rubbed my hands together with mock enthusiasm. "Mission accomplished! I don't want you distracted by all of Noah's cute friends."

Micah laughed and kissed the tip of my nose. "I'm sure I've already met most of Noah's cute friends, and they haven't *distracted* me yet. In case you haven't realized this about me, I'm not that easily distracted, with one very notable, very gorgeous, very terrific exception."

I gazed into his eyes. "I distract you?"

His expression softened. "Aww, honey, don't you realize what you do to me?" He cupped my ass and pulled me close. "You make me nuts. Ever since we met, all I've wanted to do is spend time with you. I can't stop thinking about you, don't want to sleep without you. My fingers itch to touch you whenever I see you. And when we broke up..." He shook his head and laughed ruefully. "My heart actually hurt." He looked deep into my eyes. "I really do love you, Ben Forman."

I put my hand on his chest and leaned in for a quick kiss. "I love you too. And I'm so sorry for how I acted. I didn't mean to hurt you. I just..."

He covered my hand with his and squeezed. "Don't apologize. You already explained what you were going through, and I understand. We're together now, so let's not look back. Okay?"

I nodded, feeling grateful for his understanding and trying to push away regret for things I couldn't change. There wasn't anything I could do about my past mistakes, but going forward, I could show Micah how much he meant to me. And that was exactly what I would do.

I was finally in love with someone, and I could see myself sharing my whole life with him. Micah was handsome, successful, smart, kind, funny... I could go on and on with his list of positive attributes. Feeling ashamed of being with

Micah Trains made no sense, and I was done being controlled by a fear of other people's reactions or a desire to meet other people's expectations. It was time to live *my* life in a way that felt right to *me*.

CHAPTER EIGHTEEN

IT TURNED out that Roxy's Diner was a fifties-style diner in EC West complete with red-topped metal tables, black and white checkered floors, and jukeboxes. There was also a large patio out back, and that was where we found Noah, Clark, Zach, and Aaron. They waved us over and said hello. Then Micah focused on a couple of guys I didn't recognize at the end of the table.

The older one stood as soon as he saw us approaching and smiled warmly at Micah, the sides of his brown eyes crinkling. "Micah! I didn't know you'd be here. Who finally managed to talk you into taking a morning off work and coming to brunch?"

Micah hugged the brown-haired man and then turned to me and held his hand out. Instinct honed during many years of self-preservation made me hesitate. We were at a public restaurant, outside, where anyone could see us. Straight men didn't hold hands.

Micah gave me an understanding smile and began lowering his arm. He was offering me an out, but I didn't want to take it. I wasn't straight, and there was nothing wrong with that. Yeah, I would need to play that one on auto-repeat until it finally sank in.

I rolled my shoulders and forced myself to move forward and take Micah's hand. He tried to keep his expression neutral, but I could see an extra twinkle in those blue eyes, I noticed the sides of his mouth rising just a little higher, and I was aware of a slight bit of tension easing from his shoulders.

"Ben, I want you to meet my rabbi and good friend, Seth Cohen. Seth, this is Ben Forman."

Seth clasped my hand between both of his and shook it. "Wonderful to finally meet you, Ben. I've been hearing about you for months."

Knowing that Micah had been talking about me made me feel oddly tingly. I darted my eyes toward Micah, and he shrugged. "What can I say? Seth's gifted at getting people to spill their guts. I think it might come with the job description."

The younger man who'd been sitting next to Seth stood up and joined our conversation. "Yeah, and it was like pulling teeth to get you to talk about him, Micah." Sarcasm dripped from his voice. "Almost as hard as getting you to shut the fuck up."

"And this charming specimen is Seth's partner, Eli," Micah said completely deadpan. "Way to make an impression, Eli."

I was taken aback that Micah's religious leader was gay, but I recovered quickly and remained engaged in the conversation. "Don't worry about it, Eli. I grew up with Noah, so sarcasm and cussing is like verbal comfort food to me."

"I don't know what you're talking about, Ben," my

brother interjected. "I'm as sweet and delicate as a flower." He actually batted his eyelashes, which looked ridiculous coming from such a tall, muscular, rough-looking guy. "Now sit your ass down and grab a menu, 'cause I'm hungry enough to eat the ass of a dead horse."

There was only one empty chair left at the table, so Zach jumped up from his spot and sat on Aaron's lap. "There you go, perfect amount of seating," he said.

Clark laughed and shook his head. "Sit in your own seat, Zach. I'll get Ben a chair." He turned toward Noah. "Are Bert and Ernie coming too, or do we just need seating for one more?"

"Bert and Ernie?" I asked Clark.

"They spent years playing off the whole 'we're just friends and roommates' bit, which earned them those nicknames. Thankfully, they eventually came to their senses." Clark pulled over an empty chair from the next table, and Micah and I sat down. "There we are. Zach, you can have your chair back now."

Zach scowled at Clark and wiggled around on Aaron's lap, causing the blond's cheeks to turn a distinct pink color. "I'm comfortable here. What's the big deal? It's not as if I'm straddling him or anything." He picked up his water glass and took a sip. Then a huge grin spread over his pixie face, and he jumped to his feet. "Although now that I think about it, the parts all line up just fine this way." His hand was on the button of his jeans in a second. "Unzip and whip it out, big guy, and we can have some real fun."

Was he serious? I imagined my eyes got so wide that I looked like one of those Japanese anime cartoons. How was it Zach could always make me feel like an innocent kid constantly shocked by the things that went on in the world around me?

"Aaron, you gotta do a better job keeping your man satisfied if he's this hard up," Noah said without even bothering to look up from his menu.

Zach slumped into the empty chair he had vacated. "He doesn't need any tips from you, asshole. And he's already gotten me off twice this morning, thank you very fucking much."

Aaron's ears turned red all the way to the tips, but he didn't say a word.

Clark smirked and met my eyes. "Believe it or not, Noah and Zach actually like each other."

Oh, I believed it. I was very familiar with Noah's behavior when he didn't like someone. There was nothing subtle about my brother.

"Are you boys done, or do we need to get a ruler and compare dick sizes next?" That comment came from Eli, Rabbi Seth's partner, and I thought it was about fifty-fifty whether Noah, Zach, or both would drop trou right there.

"Eli, don't encourage them." Seth looked around the table. "Have any of you ever had the french toast here?"

And with that effective diversion, everybody settled

down. We ate a hearty, greasy breakfast, chatted about nothing in particular, and just hung out. Even though I was at a table with a bunch of men whose body language left no doubt about their sexual orientation, I was comfortable. Or maybe I was comfortable *because* I was with those guys. I felt like I could be myself without being judged, and that made it possible for me to relax and not worry about every word I uttered and every gesture I made.

Eventually, people said their goodbyes and left, until Micah and I were alone with Noah and Clark.

"So did Mom and Dad totally lose their shit yesterday?" Noah asked.

"Yeah, they were pretty upset."

My brother snorted at what he knew was an understatement. "They'll never learn. Losing one son because they're assholes wasn't enough. They had to lose both of us."

Okay, coming out to my parents hadn't been great, but then again, I hadn't expected it to be. But whatever happened, they were still our parents. I hated hearing Noah talk that way about them.

"I'm done pretending to be someone I'm not, Noah, but I'm not done being their son." I dragged my fingers through my hair and then propped my elbows on the table and looked at my brother. So many years of being angry and resentful couldn't be easy on him. I wished there were a way to get Noah to give our parents another chance, but I knew that was impossible, at least until they stopped clinging to their judgmental attitudes. "Look, I'm not going to say it wouldn't have been better if they'd smiled and hugged me and said nothing had changed and I was still the same son they'd always loved, but deep down inside I think they feel that way. I just need to give them time to get used to the idea."

"You better be prepared to wait forever, Ben, because they're never gonna change," Noah said as he got up from the table. He brushed off his pants and then reached for Clark, pulling him into a hug.

My brother was right in a sense. If I didn't make an effort, then it was possible my parents' relationship with me would become just as fractured and nonexistent as their relationship with Noah. But I wasn't ready to give up on my family.

Micah got up, and we all started walking out of the patio.

"Are you going into the office today, Micah?"

"Uh-huh. Sorry, honey, but I think we've got a real chance at a settlement if we put in a bit more work right now." He put his hand on the small of my back and rubbed circles through my T-shirt.

I got a little closer to him, enjoying the warmth and contact. "That's okay. It'll give me a chance to go see my parents again. Maybe it'll be better now that they've had a chance to calm down and absorb everything."

Noah caught my eye and curled his fingers in a circle before raising his hand to his mouth and tilting his head back in a mime of taking a shot. I didn't understand what he was doing at first, but then I remembered our conversation about my stupid mistakes being a drinking game. What had I done wrong this time?

Micah and I were parked on the opposite side of the lot from Clark and Noah, so we said our goodbyes and went our separate ways.

"So what are you going to say to you parents?" Micah asked.

"Nothing brilliant. I just want them to know that I'm still here, I'm still me, and I still love them."

Suddenly, I registered my mistake. Our last big fight had been about Micah wanting to go with me when I visited my parents, and here I was intentionally planning a visit for a time when he wouldn't be available. I stopped in my tracks and clasped Micah's arm, twisting him around until we were facing each other. "Micah, please don't think that I don't want my parents to meet you. They will meet you. But I have to get things straightened out between us first. Bringing you into this right now won't be pleasant for anyone. I know that sounds like a copout or like I'm being spineless, but—"

"I wouldn't expect you to handle things any other way, Ben." I could see the sincerity in his eyes as he spoke. "They're dealing with a big shock right now, and meeting their son's boyfriend probably won't help them assimilate all this new information. If they're anything like I suspect, bringing me in will just add a visual image to something they're desperately trying to deny."

I nodded. It seemed like people who had issues with homosexuality had an unusual propensity to immediately think of sex when they came across a gay couple. That seemed counterintuitive to me, but it was true. And I had heard my father make enough disparaging comments about Noah's sex life to know he wasn't an exception.

"Yeah, that's it exactly," I said. "Plus, I don't want your first impression of them to be the way they're acting right now. I know you must already think my parents are complete jerks from the things you've heard, but they're good people, and they love me and Noah."

Micah cupped the back of my head and ran his fingers through my hair. "I don't think they sound like jerks. Despite what you might think, honey, when you talk about your parents, you always say many more good things than bad." He gazed into my eyes with an expression so full of love it almost made my knees buckle. "I admire how dedicated you are to your family. Being so loyal to people right after they've hurt you can't be easy. You know, you really sell yourself short, Ben. I think you're incredibly brave."

FOUR HOURS later, I didn't feel particularly brave. I was fully clothed, huddled underneath my comforter, soaking my pillow with tears. Needless to say I had gotten nowhere with my parents. They were still resolute in their demand that I "stop this despicable behavior and come to your senses." And the funny thing, if you could call any part of the whole situation funny, was that it was no longer my own feelings, thoughts, and behavior that I found despicable.

Somewhere along the way, I had come to terms with myself, and now my parents' behavior struck me as completely out of line and outrageous. Even though I knew they weren't acting any differently than they had my entire life.

Maybe my brother was right. Maybe it was hopeless to try to change their viewpoint on this. Maybe finding myself really did mean losing my parents. And cue the waterworks.

Let's both take a moment to be grateful that you're reading this and not actually watching it all go down, because there's nothing more pathetic than a guy in his midthirties crying over his mommy.

I must have fallen asleep at some point, because when I heard my phone ringing and poked my head out from underneath the blanket, it was pitch black. I fumbled on the nightstand and eventually brought the phone to my ear. "'Lo." Damn, did my voice sound as bad outside as it did in my head? All scratchy and sore, like I had been singing or yelling or crying. Okay, yeah, it was the last one, but I was holding out hope it wouldn't be obvious.

"Shit." It was Noah. "That bad, huh?"

There was no point in denying it. "Uh-huh."

He let out a long, loud sigh. "I'm coming with you the

next time you go over there."

"I don't think that's a good idea, Noah. They're as bad as I've ever seen them. We can't subject Clark to that."

"Not Clark. Just me."

I was shocked speechless. Noah had absolutely refused to come to any family gathering—whether a casual lunch or Christmas dinner—without Clark since the moment he came out. No, it was actually even earlier than that, probably since they started dating, but all of us thought they were just roommates.

"Why now?" I asked. "You've always insisted on bringing him. What's changed?"

Another sigh, and then, "You. You're what's changed. Look, I gave up on having any kind of decent relationship with Mom and Dad before I entered my teens. But you... I still don't think it'll work. I still think they're hateful assholes. But if you insist on trying, then I'll be right there by your side. You're my brother, and I'm not letting you do this alone."

I started blubbering again, which was even more humiliating with my tough-guy brother listening to me, but I couldn't help it. "Thanks, Noah. I didn't know if I could face them again, but if you're with me..."

"Yeah, I know. Get some sleep, Ben. I'll talk to you later this week, and we'll figure out a time to go see Mom and Dad. Good night."

"Night."

CHAPTER NINETEEN

I WISH I could tell you that having Noah come with me to see my parents fixed everything right up. But it didn't. As long as we didn't talk about our personal lives, things stayed civil. My father asked about work. My mother took an unnatural interest in the weather. And when we got to the part of the scheduled programming where Noah or I would try to get through to them about who we were, it all fell apart, and we were back to square one. The whole thing was frustrating to say the least.

Seeing as how my relationship with my parents was on life support as it was, I decided that it made sense to just pull the Band-Aid of denial off in one fast motion. So I made plans with the guy in my circle of friends who found it damn near impossible to keep any sort of secret under wraps and explained why I would no longer be bringing women to parties or going trolling with him at bars. My cell phone was ringing before I made it home that night, and I confirmed the information to a few more people. I figured that'd be the end of it, I had come out. After that, none of my friends raised a fuss, for the most part. But there were definitely a few exceptions.

I was at my buddy Neil's house about a week later for a bi-monthly poker game he held. It might have been my imagination that a couple of guys had trouble making eye contact with me or that the people in the kitchen got unusually quiet when I walked into the room. But paranoia could not explain the snide remarks Tristan kept muttering *almost* under his breath.

"Oh, I better be careful about bending over like that around Ben" after he picked up a card that he dropped on the floor.

"This isn't an invitation" when he walked by the chair where I was sitting and brought his crotch oddly close to my face.

And then, apropos of nothing at all, "You marched in any parades lately, Benny boy?"

It took a great deal of self-restraint for me not to slam my cards down on the table before I got up and walked out of the room. Dealing with those types of comments was new for me, and I wasn't sure how to respond without getting into a fight or inciting even more nasty remarks.

I had barely made it to the entryway when I felt a hand on my shoulder. I spun around and tightened my fists at my sides, wishing for the first time that I had asked my brother to teach me one or two of his kickboxing moves.

Neil's arms flew up, and he took a step back. "Hey, stand down, man. I was just coming to ask if you're okay."

I took a deep breath. "Yeah, I'm fine. But I'm leaving."

Neil shook his head. "Please don't. Look, Ben, Tristan's an asshole. You know that. Just ignore him."

I dragged my fingers through my hair in frustration. "Yeah, I know. But I'm not going to be the butt of his jokes all night."

"So you're just going to let him push you out of here? That's exactly what he wants, you know."

Yeah, Neil was right. And I didn't want to give that smug bastard the satisfaction of knowing he'd succeeded. "Okay, fine. I'll go back in there, but I'm done taking Tristan's crap."

Neil covered his mouth with his hand and tried to hold back a laugh.

"What?" I asked. He shook his head. "What?" I repeated more loudly.

"Nothing, it's just..." He laughed again. "If you go in there and talk about 'taking his crap' and being the 'butt of his jokes,' he might implode from all the gay joke opportunities."

I smacked Neil's shoulder. "Very nice, Neil. I thought you were on my side here." My smile took the sting out of my words. Frankly, I was relieved that I could have a conversation with at least one old friend without feeling uncomfortable. "All right, let's go back in there."

We hadn't even gotten far enough into the room to take our seats when Tristan got back to his commentary, no longer bothering with any pretense of subtlety.

"Are you feeling better now, Ben? I bet it had to hurt

to sit down for so long considering what you take up your ass nowadays."

I stumbled to a halt, trying to formulate some sort of response, but Neil beat me to it.

"You have a lot of experience getting fucked up the ass, Tristan? No? Then keep your helpful insight to yourself."

Drunk-as-usual Clayton joined in. "I used to date a chick that liked to take it in the back door," he slurred. "And she never had any problem sitting around after." He took a swig of his beer and then quickly set it down, causing it to tip and splash on the table. "And it ain't 'cause I'm small, neither. I'd whip it out to show you that I'm packin', but I'm a grow-er not a show-er, so..." He finished his thought with a shrug and drained the rest of his beer.

Tristan scowled at Clayton and then looked around the table. "So we're all just going to sit here and pretend like everything's normal? Doesn't it bother any of you that Ben's suddenly decided to start fucking guys?"

Jack, who was usually a reserved, goes-to-church-on-Sundays, has-a-wife-and-three-kids-and-coaches-kids'-football type of man, apparently decided he'd had enough of the entire conversation, because he glared at Tristan and raised his voice for what might have been the first time in his life. "I don't care who Ben's fucking, but I do care who I'm fucking, and if I don't get home at a reasonable hour tonight, that'll be nobody. I have no interest in spending the night on the couch, so let's stop talking about Ben's love life and start focusing on cards."

That seemed to do the trick, because everybody settled down, and we played poker.

DESPITE ALL the family pain and the awkwardness with my friends, I was still happier than I ever had been in my life. I was spending a lot of time with my brother, connecting in a way that we never had as kids. I made new friends, many of whom I met through Noah or Micah. And even though I hadn't known them long, I felt closer to my new friends than I did to the guys I had been hanging around with for years. Plus, I reconnected with an old friend—Clark and I were almost as tight as we had been when we were younger.

Put that together with the fact that my stomach no longer felt like it was eating itself due to constant anxiety, and it would have been enough to make me glad I had finally taken ownership and control of my life. And then there was Micah. Sharp as a whip, sexy as sin, and one hundred percent mine.

He was working like a dog, getting ready for his upcoming trial while simultaneously trying to broker some kind of settlement and managing the rest of his case load. I think the man billed more hours during that three-month period than some lawyers did in half the year. But through it all, he made time for me.

Most evenings he pulled himself away from the office to have dinner with me, and at least a couple of days a week he shut down and got home at a reasonable hour so we could spend the night together. Well, I thought we were spending the night together. The reduction in my stress level had a proportionate impact on my ability to sleep soundly, which meant I fell asleep and stayed that way until morning. Especially when I was in Micah's bed.

But on the second Sunday in September, I woke up in the middle of the night to use the bathroom and noticed that Micah's side of the bed was empty. After draining my bladder, I stumbled out of the bathroom to go look for him. A sliver of light leaking from underneath the door to his home office told me exactly where to find my wayward boyfriend.

I turned the knob and pushed the door open. Micah was sprawled on the ground, surrounded by papers. I blinked my eyes rapidly, trying to get used to the suddenly bright light. "What're you doing? How long have you been up?"

Micah's head jerked up. "Oh! You startled me." He jumped to his feet and rushed over to me, then rubbed his hands over the sides of my arms at a rapid pace. "Did I wake you, honey? I'm sorry." The words raced out of his mouth.

My eyes had finally adjusted to the light, and I looked around the room, noticing an empty coffee carafe. It looked like a twelve cup. Maybe fourteen. "Since when do you drink coffee?"

He shrugged and shifted from foot to foot. Not like he was nervous, more like he couldn't stay still. "I get more bang for my buck than with the tea this way. It's been helping me stay up."

"How long have you been doing this?" I asked, and then I shook my head. It didn't matter. "Micah, it's like one in the morning or something. Can you stop for the night and come to bed?"

Those now familiar arms wrapped around me and pulled me close. I could feel his heart racing, and his breath was hitting my neck in an unusually fast clip. "I don't think I can sleep just yet." His head snapped back, and he looked at me. "Hey, can I show you something? I think I've figured out how to settle this thing before the trial starts on Wednesday, but I need a second set of eyes."

I dipped my head forward and kissed his soft lips. My hands found their way to his cheeks, and I stroked his beard. "Sure. But just remember that my last involvement with anything litigation related was in moot court during law school, and the only thing I know about your case is what you've told me and what I've heard people say here and there around the office."

He nodded, the pace so unnaturally fast that his head bobbed like one of those ridiculous dolls they hand out at baseball games. "Yeah, okay. So you know how our guy denies that he had an offer to sell the company until *after* the plaintiff had already told him that he wanted to terminate their partnership? But the plaintiff, our guy's former business partner, claims the offer came in like a month before he ever talked about leaving and that our guy hid it from him and then conned him into selling at rock-bottom price so our guy could turn around and sell it to the buyer and pocket the whole windfall?"

"Uh huh." That much I knew. Our client had created some sort of irrigation supply company with one of his classmates from graduate school. Ten years later, they were doing really well, and the business partner wanted to get out of the industry. They came to an agreement on price, and our client bought his partner out. A month later there was some shift in the industry, and a bigger company came in and made our client an offer worth ten times as much as what he had spent to buy out his partner. Our guy sold, his former business partner heard about the deal, and litigation ensued.

"So every letter and calendar entry is dated at least a month after our client had bought out his partner. Plus the new owner confirms our timeline. But we keep getting tripped up because of this e-mail we found when we were pulling all sorts of communication during discovery. We were required to disclose it, so we did, and it's been killing our case ever since." Micah dropped to the ground and sifted through the papers, finding the one he wanted and then handing it to me. "See? It's dated thirty-two days before our client bought out his partner, and it says that he was approached by the buyer to sell the company. It even has the offering price. The plaintiff says he wasn't told about this and, if he had been, he'd have waited a month and sold right along with our client so he could make more money."

"Okay. So what'd you find?" Honestly, I questioned whether Micah was even capable of logical thought in his current state. I had never seen anyone so hopped up on caffeine.

"Well, the subject line in that e-mail has always bothered me. Supposedly the client was writing to his wife with this great news about how they were going to make all sorts of money. And the subject line is…"

I looked at the e-mail and read the subject line out loud. "One more thing."

Again with the bobblehead nod. "Yeah. That's weird, right? I mean, they're about to make enough money to retire and travel the globe or buy a mansion, or, hell, both, and that's just one more thing? Doesn't make sense."

"Okay. I can see that, I guess. But the body of this e-mail is pretty clear, Micah. So's the date. And if it came from your client's computer…"

Micah sat down and patted the spot next to him. "True enough. But it still bothered me, so I met with the IT guys last week and talked to them about their system. Turns out they back everything up at the end of the week in an offsite location. I asked them to find the backup tapes from this time period and send me all the e-mails our client sent or received. Take a look at this."

He handed me another e-mail. It was from our client to his wife, just like the previous e-mail. It had the same date, time, and subject line. But the body was completely different.

"This is about how he's going to be working late so he'll have to meet her at this dinner, or whatever, that night," I summarized.

"Exactly! Same subject, same date and time, totally different body. So I got to thinking, maybe someone messed with the e-mail after he sent it." His eyes were wide with excitement, and his pupils were dilated. I needed to hide the coffee maker.

"Is that possible?" I asked calmly.

"On Outlook it is. I tested it. You can go into your sent e-mails and edit one of them, then save it, and it shows up with the same date and time and no way to know that it was changed after the fact. But that doesn't change anything in the backups they make, because they're stored apart from the regular system."

Well, Micah was jittery and high on caffeine, but it sounded like he had made a major breakthrough in the case. Of course he had. The man was a genius. It was one of the things that attracted me to him, along with his drive and determination. But that didn't mean I was going to watch him work himself into the ground.

"I think you're onto something. Of course you still need to figure out how someone got into our client's e-mail so they could change it, but it seems pretty clear that this e-mail he supposedly sent to his wife isn't real."

"Yeah, that's what I was going to do next," he said as he looked around the room, clearly trying to decide where to start with that task.

I took his hand in mine and tugged him toward the door. "Not tonight, you're not. You've already done the hard part. Tomorrow you can figure out the other details. Right now, you need some rest."

"Honestly, Ben, I think I'm too wound up to sleep."

Well, that wasn't going to dissuade me. I got us to the door and turned off the light. "Let me worry about that." I turned back and kissed him gently. "I think I've picked up some good ideas on how to relax you over the past few months."

CHAPTER TWENTY

DESPITE HIS predisposition to work constantly, Micah followed me without any further complaint. By the time we got to the bedroom, his chest was pressed up against my back and he was licking my ear and groping whatever parts of my body he could reach.

"Six," he mumbled into my neck.

"What?"

"We've been seeing each other for almost six months."

He was right. Our first dinner together had been in early April, and it was already mid-September. In some ways, the time had flown by. But in other ways, when I looked back at my life back then, it seemed like it belonged to somebody else, like I had been somebody else. I guessed in some ways I had been somebody else; I had been the person everyone expected me to be. And now, I was me.

I kept walking until we were in the bathroom, and then I twisted around and pushed Micah's sweatpants down and yanked his T-shirt off. I hadn't bothered getting dressed when I had gone searching for him, so that was all it took for us to be skin to skin from head to toe and everywhere in between. Our lips met, and the kiss was instantly intense.

Micah's tongue invaded my mouth, his hands grasped my ass, and that wiry body ground against mine.

"I love you so much," he panted into my mouth. "Want you all the time." His hips thrust forward. "I have this reoccurring fantasy whenever you walk into my office where I close the door, drop to me knees, and...oh, hell, I'll show you."

And with that, he lowered his body until he was kneeling on the bathmat, and then he nuzzled my groin. He burrowed his nose in the crease of my leg and then dragged it over my balls, inhaling deeply. "Love how you smell," he whimpered before continuing his exploration. His tongue joined the party, licking my sac and the base of my cock. Eventually, he stopped licking and started sucking, taking first one round orb into his mouth and then the other.

I groaned and clasped his head, holding him close to me. "Micah, ugh, touch my dick," I begged and then trembled when he did just that, his fingers surprisingly gentle when he traced the vein on the underside of my cock.

He moved his head up and licked my glans with light swipes, ratcheting my arousal higher, but not enough to get me release. I increased the pressure on the back of his head, urging him forward. "Suck me. Please."

I heard him chuckle before his mouth opened, and he swallowed me down, surrounding my dick in wet warmth. He kept his lips gripped tightly around my dick and moved down until my crown was nudging the back of his throat.

Then he pulled back up before dropping forward again.

"That's so good." I looked down and met his eyes. His lips were stretched wide around my cock, saliva pooling on the sides, slicking his way up and down my dick. His blue eyes were hot with lust, and his hand was wrapped around his own dick, stroking in time with his sucks on mine.

The visual alone almost made me lose it. But that wasn't how I wanted to come, so I pushed his head back. He groaned in frustration, which made a new surge of lust shoot through me. I loved how much he enjoyed going down on me, how much he enjoyed every aspect of our sex life. And he wasn't alone. I was endlessly grateful that his house was on a big lot, because he regularly made me come so hard that I screamed loud enough to shake the windows.

"I want you inside me," I explained as I turned around and leaned over the counter, tilting my ass up in invitation.

"Fuck, you're hot." Micah's hand caressed my firm globes. Then he stood and blanketed my body with his, kissing my neck and shoulders.

I rested my cheek against the countertop and closed my eyes. Micah retrieved the bottle of lube we kept in the shower. I heard the cap snap open seconds before a slick finger circled my puckered opening. My legs instinctively spread wider, making room for my lover. One finger pushed inside me, and then Micah's hand was on my lower back and his cock was at my entrance. We had stopped using condoms the day our tests came back clean, which helped add a certain level of spontaneity to our sex life.

"Ready?" he asked breathlessly.

"God, yes."

He pushed in slowly, not stopping, not speeding up, just stretching my channel with his thick dick until his balls were squished up against my ass. He hesitated for just a moment, and then he pulled out and pushed back in again, faster this time. I moaned, letting him know that was what I wanted—a hard, fast fuck.

Micah seemed to understand, because that was exactly what he gave me. His hands gripped my hips as he relentlessly pounded into my body. I loved that feeling, the slight ache inside mixed with the unparalleled pleasure. I enjoyed topping Micah, but being on the receiving end was just as good.

"I'm close, honey. Can you touch yourself?" That gravelly voice was tight with barely tethered restraint.

I pushed back to make room between my cock and the counter, then snaked my hand underneath and circled my dick in a firm grip. It didn't take much stimulation, not with Micah dragging his dick over my prostate as he pummeled my channel.

"Micah! Oh, God, yes!" I shouted as I shot strings of ejaculate onto the vanity and floor beneath me.

"Ungh, yeah," he moaned, keeping hold of my hip with one hand and my shoulder with his other as he pushed all the way inside me and stilled.

I looked into the mirror and gasped at the sight. Micah's head was thrown back, the veins on the sides of this throat were bulging, his mouth was hanging open, and his eyes were clenched shut. If ever there was a picture of ecstasy, it was my lover in the throes of an orgasm.

When his dick stopped pulsing, he collapsed on top of me, his forehead resting between my shoulder blades as he gasped to get air into his lungs. I enjoyed his weight on my body, so I didn't ask him to move. Eventually, both of our pulse rates slowed, and we got up.

"Okay, that was step one in my plan to relax you. How am I doing so far?"

He rubbed his hand over the top of his head. "Step one? Fuck! How many steps are there in this plan of yours, honey? 'Cause I'm an old man, and any more than what we did just might kill me."

I put my arms around his waist and gave him a tight hug. "Don't worry, old man. I'll give you enough time to recover. You start the bath and I'll get us some water. We need to get some hydration into your caffeine stream."

I was almost out the door when Micah called my name. I turned around and met his tender gaze.

"Thanks for taking care of me, Ben."

My chest tightened and my heart stuttered. "Always."

"SO I was thinking of going to LA at the end of the month for Rosh Hashana," Micah said.

I was sitting at the end of the bathtub, leaning against the glass tiles, with my arms wrapped around Micah, who was lying between my legs with his head resting on my shoulder and his hands stroking my thighs and knees. The steam and the quiet were having the intended relaxing effect on me, and based on Micah's slowed speech pattern, I thought he was finally winding down.

"Mmm. Which one's Rosh Hashana again?"

"Jewish New Year. It's not super time-consuming, just a few hours in temple the first night and again the next morning. But it'll be nice to see my family, and if the trial settles, we could make it a longer trip. Maybe two weeks, and then we'll be there for Yom Kippur too."

Okay, that woke me up. "We?"

Micah tilted his head back and kissed my chin. "Uh-huh. *We*. I'd like you to meet my family, and I want them to meet you. What do you think?"

"I think it sounds like you're pretty serious about me," I teased.

"Don't bust my balls about this, Benjamin."

I dragged my hands across his chest, over his stomach, and down to his groin, where I cupped his soft cock and balls. "Oh, now you know I'd never hurt your balls. I love playing with them far too much."

"You're not funny," he grumbled.

"I beg to differ. I think I'm pretty friggin' hilarious."

He sighed. "Whatever. So are you gonna come meet my family?"

I was having too much fun to stop playing with him. "That depends. You didn't answer my question."

"What's your damn question?" Growly Micah was just as adorable as regular Micah.

"My question..." I gave his package a final squeeze and then ran my fingers back up his body and played with the hair on his chest. "Is whether the invitation means you're serious about me?"

Micah suddenly pulled away, splashing water over the side of the tub. At first I thought I had pushed him too far and he was pissed. But then he twisted his body around so he was facing me and rose so his left foot was planted on the bottom of the tub along with his right knee. He reached for my hand and yanked it toward him, resting it on his elevated knee.

"I was going to wait until after the trip so my mother wouldn't kill me for doing this with a guy she's never met, but you leave me no choice. Ehm, Ben Forman, will you make me the happiest guy on earth and become my domestic partner?"

I couldn't hold back my laugh. "You did *not* just ask me to be your domestic partner. Was that supposed to be some kind of proposal? 'Cause I've gotta tell you, Micah, it was seriously lacking in the romance department."

"Hey, you can blame our political leaders for that. As soon as they pull their heads out of their collective asses and overturn DOMA, we can get hitched and have it mean something. But for now, domestic partners is the best I can do."

I flipped my hand over so I could get a grip on his wrist, and then I pulled him forward until he toppled and landed with his chest against mine. "You're such a lawyer," I said as I stroked his cheek.

"Yeah, I am." He leaned forward and kissed me, taking my bottom lip between both of his and tugging it gently before pulling away. "But I'm also a guy who is ass over teakettle in love with you. If you want romance, I'll buy you flowers or get candles or...hell, I'll fuckin' Google 'romantic gestures' first thing in the morning and follow every damn suggestion, just..." He sighed deeply. "Ben, I love you. I mean, I really, really love you."

It was hard to breathe after that little speech, and I couldn't blink fast enough to keep the tears from leaking out of the corners of my eyes. "I love you too, Micah," I whispered to him. "Yes, I'll come meet your family. And yes, I'll move in with you. But the 'happiest guy on earth' title is off the table, because as of this moment, it belongs to me."

CHAPTER TWENTY-ONE

YOU'D THINK given the late—or was it early?—hour, I would have been asleep the second my head hit the pillow. But as it turned out, helping Micah relax and unwind had ended up getting certain parts of me all worked up. More specifically, my heart, which actually ached as a result of the depth of my feelings for Micah, and my dick, which was about the furthest thing possible from relaxed, again, because of those feelings.

Don't get me wrong, I wasn't complaining. Great sex was worth a sleepless night any day of the week and twice on Sunday. So I figured I would go for middle-of-the-night orgasm number two.

"Micah?"

"Mmm-hmm."

"On Thursday night when you were working late, I was home alone and I was bored and, um, horny so I..."

He sat up, letting the blanket pool around his waist. From the expression on his face, it was clear that I had gotten his attention. "Yeah?"

"I thought it might be, uh, nice to watch some porn. So I went online and I saw something that I wanna try."

"Yes," he agreed with a firm nod.

"You didn't even hear what it is yet."

"You said porn, right?" he responded. "As far as I'm concerned, anything that involves getting sweaty and sticky with you goes on the 'yes' list. No questions asked."

I smiled at him and circled the perimeter of his nipple with the tip of my index finger. "Ditto."

"Hmmm, a fantasy swap. This could be like the best version ever of 'you show me yours and I'll show you mine.'"

Just the thought of hearing Micah tell me one of his fantasies was enough to make me moan out loud. "Yeah, you're on," I said, before pulling him down and pressing close to his body.

We lay on our sides, our hands exploring each other as our tongues danced. I ran my fingers through Micah's chest hair, pulling on the soft strands just enough to make him groan. After that, I reached lower and cupped his cock, feeling the silky skin covering hard steel. I curled my fingers around his erection and slid my fist up and down. Micah decided to get in on that action and took my dick into his hand, jacking me in concert with my movement around his hard member.

"It always amazes me how much better it feels to have your hand on me than my own," I mumbled into his mouth.

"Mmm-hmm." He tilted his head, taking our kiss deeper and sucking my tongue harder.

I knew that if we didn't stop soon, it would all be over, so I reluctantly pulled away. "Flip onto your stomach for me."

No question, no complaint, just immediate compliance as Micah wiggled a little and got onto his stomach and rested his arms at his sides. I straddled his thighs and flattened my hand on his back, running it over the smooth skin, feeling the wiry muscles bunch beneath my touch. Just that simple act—looking at my lover, touching his body—had me hard enough to pound nails. And now I was going to have this every day. I closed my eyes and thanked the universe for letting Micah Trains walk into my life.

I had promised Micah total relaxation, so I thought starting with a massage would do the trick. After retrieving a bottle of lotion from the nightstand, I coated my fingers and palms and began with his neck and shoulders, rubbing the muscles until all the tension eased from his body. Micah remained still beneath me except for the occasional wiggle and more-than-occasional groan of satisfaction. Those groans sounded an awful lot like sex noises, so by the time I reached his lower back, I was done with the massage and ready to move on to something a little more X-rated.

I caressed the mounds of his ass and scooted down a bit farther, wedging myself between Micah's legs. Then I bent forward and placed a small kiss at the base of Micah's spine, right above his ass. That kiss led to another just a bit lower, and soon my hands shifted from caressing Micah's ass to pulling those cheeks apart and exposing his cleft.

My fingers explored first, running over the normally hidden skin and making Micah tremble. And then I dipped my face forward and let my tongue follow the same path.

"Ben!" Micah shouted my name and brought his knees up and out so his ass was elevated and available to me.

"You like this?" I asked him before leaning down to take a long swipe from his balls up to the edge of his crack.

"Yeah, ungh! Yes, I like it. Don't stop."

I had no intention of stopping. The flavor and scent of my lover, the sound of his pleasure, the feel of his body, all those things had me just as worked up as Micah. I stopped talking and concentrated on Micah's body. Long licks gave way to short swipes focused more and more on his rosebud until eventually, I was circling that puckered opening with my tongue and then pressing my way inside.

"Oh, God," Micah moaned. "Feels good."

It was good for me too. I wiggled my tongue just on the inside of his body, then pulled it out and licked around his opening again, before darting back inside. Eventually, my lips were pressed tight against him and my tongue was buried all the way inside, plunging in and out of his ass.

I needed to get inside that hot body so desperately I was shaking. I moved back onto my knees and grabbed the bottle of lotion that was still lying next to me. It would have to do instead of lube. No way did I have the presence of mind to go in search of anything at that moment. I coated my cock and leaned over Micah, my left hand flat on the mattress next to him and my right hand gripping my hard cock and positioning it at his entrance.

Micah pushed back as I moved forward, and I broke through that ring of muscle easily, entering the welcoming warmth of his body. I stilled when I was balls deep, dropping my forehead onto Micah's shoulder and willing myself to calm down so it wouldn't be over before it started. Once I thought I had at least a modicum of control, I raised my hips, pulling my cock almost completely out of his ass before slamming back down again.

"Yes!" he shouted and met my thrusts, moving his hips up as I pushed down.

We found our rhythm, our bodies rocking together in concert, the pleasure almost overwhelming in its intensity. Micah folded his elbows so they supported his elevated body, and I reached my right hand underneath him, taking hold of his erection and stroking him off in time with our thrusting motions.

"I'm right there, Ben. Right there. Right there." His head shot up, neck stretched, and I felt his cock pulse and spill over my hand. "Fuck, yes!"

He was still shaking when I found my release and shot deep inside his body. After a few seconds, we both collapsed, shifting onto our sides. I tucked one arm under Micah's neck and draped the other over his waist as I pressed my chest to his back.

"Shit, honey, you should watch porn more often," he said breathlessly. "I think I'm gonna buy you a subscription for your birthday."

I laughed and kissed his neck. "Stop working so damn hard and we can watch it together."

He was quiet for a couple of minutes, but once our breathing slowed to normal, his hand covered mine and gave me a squeeze. "Just let me get this one case handled and you've got yourself a deal. With a man like you waiting for me at home, it'd be a crime to keep spending so much time at the office."

BECAUSE OF how busy Micah had been preparing for his trial, our only time together in the office had been after hours when we walked to get dinner. As a result, nobody saw us with one another enough to realize there was anything going on between us. Well, that was about to change.

Micah spent most of Monday morning and early afternoon at his client's office. And if the excited buzz on the litigation side of the floor was any indication, I guessed that he had confirmed his suspicions about the "smoking gun" e-mail being a fake. We hadn't talked about a specific time frame for me to move into his place, but I found myself so happy and excited at the prospect of spending every night with Micah and waking up in his arms every morning that I decided there was no point in delaying it.

With his case in a fever-pitch mode and him trying to broker a settlement at the eleventh hour, I figured Micah wouldn't leave the office until very late that night. Well, if I was going to be alone that evening anyway, I might as well use it productively and pack. Of course that meant getting boxes, which meant leaving the office before the truck rental and packing supplies store closed. Okay, they probably stayed open until nine, but I couldn't concentrate on work anyway, and I wanted to get my packing done so I could bring my things over to Micah's house that weekend. With my decision made, I closed the document I was working on and walked over to Micah's office to say goodnight.

He was hunched over his desk with a pen in his mouth and his hand on his head, concentrating on a document. I paused at his doorway and looked my fill. Short brown hair, brow creased in concentration, full lips, and even though I couldn't see them, I knew there were intelligent blue eyes to go with that package. My body instinctively moved toward my sexy lover.

"Hey." He smiled up at me as soon as he heard me approach.

"Hey, yourself." I kept walking until I was right next to him, but I still didn't feel close enough.

Micah must have felt the same way, because he rolled his chair back and patted his lap.

I sat down, circled my arms around his neck, and rested my chin on his shoulder. "So what'd you find out this morning? Do you think you have what you need to get your case settled?"

Micah kissed my cheek and rubbed my back. "Yup. I interviewed every staff member at the client's office who had access to his e-mail. His secretary started bawling after two minutes. Turns out the plaintiff was so sure our client had been trying to cut him out of the sale that he approached the secretary and offered to give her a portion of his winnings from the lawsuit if she'd look through e-mails to find proof that our client had been working on the deal before the partner got bought out. When she couldn't find any proof, she created it herself by editing that e-mail. She said she regretted doing it and would have eventually gone in and just deleted the thing, but before she could, we had our disclosure deadline, and we found the e-mail and turned it over to the other side."

I hugged Micah even tighter. It was a great catch on his part, and I was proud of him. "So what now?" I asked.

"Now I stay up all night and draft a letter convincing the plaintiff that walking away from this lawsuit with nothing is preferable to facing a counterclaim for malicious prosecution and falsifying evidence because he was conspiring with that employee." Another kiss to my forehead, and then Micah whispered in my ear, "I'm sorry that I won't be able to spend any time with you tonight. Soon, though. I promise once this is over, my evenings will belong to you."

I wasn't upset. After all, I understood the pressures of his job. "Don't worry about it. I need to get my stuff packed anyway, so this'll give me a chance to get it done without you around as a constant"—I kissed his nose—"delicious"—I kissed his cheek—"hot as hell"—I kissed his chin—"distraction." A soft peck on his lips, and then I pulled away before things got out of hand. "Do you want any kitchen stuff or anything else from my place, or should I just bring my clothes and personal things to your house and donate the rest to charity?"

"You can bring anything you want. If I need to get rid of some of my stuff to make room, that's fine. I want you to feel comfortable there, honey, because it's *our* house now."

A noise from the doorway got our attention. I turned my head and jumped to my feet when I saw Lanie Jorgens, one of the other litigation partners in the firm, standing just inside the threshold of Micah's office and watching us.

"Please, don't stop on my account," she said. "You're giving me enough fantasy material to last a hell of a long time."

"If you're that hard up, Lanie, it's time for you to go out and meet a man," Micah responded, completely unfazed by both her comment and the fact that she had caught us in a somewhat compromising position.

Well, it wasn't technically a compromising position. We weren't making out, and we were in Micah's private office. Plus, we were going to move in together. No reason to hide anything.

Geez, I had thought I was done with the whole coming out anxiety, and there it was rearing its head again. Well, it probably wouldn't be the last time either, but it did feel easier this time. I reached over and took Micah's hand in mine. He smiled at me, the sides of his eyes crinkling in a breath-stealing way.

"You introduce me to a straight guy that looks like either of you two"—Lanie pointed her finger and moved it back and forth between us as she spoke—"and isn't intimidated by a woman who uses her head for something other than a decorative accessory, and I'll get right on that. Until then, images of the two of you bumping uglies will have to be enough." She plopped down in one of the empty chairs facing Micah's desk and leaned back. "So, did I hear you say something about moving in together? Any chance I can get some cameras installed in your bedroom like in those reality TV shows? Just for my own personal viewing pleasure, of course."

Lanie was just the first person at work to hear our good news. The following morning, it was the firm's HR administrator when I went in to ask for paperwork notifying them about my change of address information. Of course that meant I also had to tell my secretary, because her feelings would be hurt if she heard about my relationship from somebody else at the office before I told her myself.

And by Tuesday afternoon, when we were at happy hour with most of the people from our office celebrating Micah's success in settling his case, one of the senior attorneys in my section walked up, coughed before looking anywhere but in my eyes, and mumbled, "I hear congratulations are in order so, uh, you make a lovely couple." Yeah, it was awkward as hell, but it was also well-intentioned and nice.

I probably shouldn't have expected a fire and brimstone speech from anyone at a firm that had hired Tucker Jones, an openly gay associate, and Micah, who was openly gay and our highest-grossing partner, but my self-flagellation had known no bounds, and I had spent many years being certain that other people would hate me as much as I had hated myself if they found out I was gay. So getting acceptance and even support from my colleagues was a huge relief.

CHAPTER TWENTY-TWO

I DIDN'T know if it was excitement over winning his case or the conversation we'd been having about how far along I had gotten in my packing the prior evening— hell, it could have just been hormones—but Micah had my back against the door and his mouth latched onto my neck as soon as we walked into the bedroom.

He helped me undress in a "get those clothes off before I rip them off" kind of way, and then he pushed me onto the bed and swallowed my cock.

"Oh! Christ, Micah!"

There was no warm-up, no time for my brain to process where I was going, I was just plunged straight into an incredible blow job and a rapidly approaching orgasm. I clutched the back of his head and pumped my hips up, pushing my cock farther into his mouth and throat. The rough treatment didn't bother Micah. In fact, I was pretty sure I heard happy moans coming from around my spit-slicked cock.

"Yes, suck my dick," I demanded as my hips flew up and my cock plunged balls deep into his mouth. "Take it, Micah, take it. Ungh, yes! Take my load."

My entire body stiffened and arched, with only my shoulders and ankles touching the mattress as I shot down his throat. Micah swallowed every last drop before licking me clean. When my body stopped trembling with aftershocks from the powerful orgasm, I tugged on Micah's ear. "Come up here. You melted me, and I wanna suck you too."

He crawled over my body and kneeled above me, straddling my shoulders as he unfastened his pants just enough to set his hard dick free. It found my waiting mouth like a divining rod.

Micah held onto the base of his cock and fed it to me, looking into my eyes as my mouth stretched around his wide, hard dick. There was something particularly sordid about that position, lying flat on my back, completely naked, with my almost-fully-clothed lover pinning me to the bed and watching me as he fucked my mouth. And I found it erotic as hell.

Micah pulled his dick out of my mouth slowly, then rubbed the wet head over my lips, chin, and both cheeks before shoving it back inside. "Fuck! You look so good with your lips wrapped around my dick." He pulled back until I was swirling my tongue around just his glans. Then he plunged in until he was pressing against my throat. "You like that, honey? Like sucking me off?"

I did like it, and I liked the dirty talk too. The whole scene was so arousing that my dick was somehow making an incredibly fast recovery. I wrapped my hand around my hardening member and stroked myself as Micah continued to take control of my mouth.

"It's so good with you, Ben." His words came out in breathless gasps. "Always so good with you."

Just a little more time and a little more stimulation and I knew I would be going off again. The realization excited me further. I increased the pressure of my sucks, moaned around his dick, and pumped my hips, pushing my own dick through my fist.

"Oh, yeah," he rasped. "You like this. So fucking hot."

He pushed farther into my throat, almost making me gag, before backing off and then pushing back in again. After several repetitions of that pattern, he took his cock out of my mouth and rubbed it on my face again.

"So gorgeous. Gonna come all over your face." His voice was husky and low, full of arousal and promise.

I whimpered and thrust my hips up and down, increasing the pace of my strokes.

"You want that, Ben? Want my seed all over your handsome face?"

Formulating a verbal response was impossible, but I nodded and grunted and opened my mouth, hoping that'd show him how much I wanted him to spill all over me.

Those blue eyes burned as he leaned above my face, his hand flying around his dick. "Here it comes. Here it comes." His head tilted back, but his eyes remained focused on me, and then long streams of ejaculate shot out of his cock onto my lips and cheeks.

I closed my eyes as my own orgasm hit, coating my hand in wet warmth. I felt Micah's fingers softly mapping my face, rubbing in his seed. When I finally opened my eyes, his adoring gaze greeted me.

"I've never done anything like that," he whispered.

"Me neither." My voice was just as quiet.

His eyes dipped and then he raised them to meet mine again. "I liked it."

He sounded so shy, which struck me as funny after how aggressive he had just been. I chuckled.

"I liked it too," I responded. "Guess we have some new things we can explore together, huh?"

His lips met mine with a soft kiss, and then I felt his tongue dart out, licking his own flavor off me. So hot.

"Well, we've got a lifetime together. Good to know we can keep it interesting."

I CUT out of work a little early on Friday and went back to my condo to do the last of the packing. The prospect of starting the next phase of my life—the one I shared with Micah—had me so excited that I had been able to think of little else. After talking about current market conditions with Micah's friend David—strike that, *our* friend David—who was a Realtor, I decided to rent out my condo instead of selling it.

I had also taken a careful inventory of Micah's furniture and décor. It wasn't just the architectural style of his house that was decidedly modern; the same was true for the interior space. I really liked how it looked and saw no point in changing it just so I could stand on principle and say half my furniture needed to be there too. So I picked a few pieces that I thought might add rather than detract from the design and decided to leave the rest in my condo.

Renting my place out furnished would garner a bit more rent every month, according to the Realtor I hired to find me a tenant. I wanted to use David, but he worked mainly in EC West and Central, and my condo in EC North was far enough away that he thought it would make more sense for me to hire someone who specialized in the area. The idea was sound. But the execution had an unfortunate unintended consequence.

I was going through my bathroom cabinets, packing extra toiletries and wondering whether it was possible for those little hotel sample-sized body gel bottles to reproduce, because there was no other explanation for why I had so damn many of them, when my phone rang. It was my mother, and I suddenly realized that I hadn't talked to her in close to two weeks, which was longer than I usually let things go before I touched base. Enter guilt, stage right.

"Hi, Mom."

"Ben, hi. Uh, are you home, dear? Because your father and I are right down the street, and we'd like to come see you."

Wow. That was as close to stopping by uninvited as my mother had ever come. Sure, she called first, but still. I was so happy at the prospect that my parents missed me and wanted to spend time with me, that maybe they finally accepted me as I was, that I didn't think about the boxes strewn about my living room. "Sure. Come on over."

I had just enough time to toss out the fitness magazines that doubled for porn I had left on my counter to show Micah. When I came across them while packing up my bedroom, I thought it would be a funny little anecdote to share with him, a "look how far I've come" kind of moment. But then I decided I didn't want him looking at other men, even if they were Photoshopped images of people he would never meet in real life. Huh, I never realized I had a jealous streak. Well, I had never been with someone I wanted to keep, someone I loved.

The knock on my door disrupted my mental musings, which was probably a good thing.

Come on, don't act surprised. You've gotten a glimpse inside my mind. You know how unbalanced things are in there.

"Hi, Mom. Hi, Dad. Come on in."

I held the door open for my parents as they walked into my condo. The place wasn't very big, and the front door opened to the combination entryway/living room/dining room. All the furniture was still there, so there wasn't an issue with places to sit. But I knew I would have to explain the boxes lined up against the wall.

My father looked around the room and then glared at me. "So it's true." He sounded angry. "Helga from my office said her husband's real estate firm is listing your condo. Can you imagine how embarrassed I was when she realized I didn't even know my own son was moving?"

In the span of just a few days, I had agreed to move in with Micah and made all the necessary arrangements. Somehow, calling my parents to share the good news hadn't made it onto my to-do list. The realization saddened me, because it highlighted just how far apart we had drifted. But there was nothing more I could do to solve that problem.

Noah and I were still having the occasional dinner with them. The get-togethers were strained and unpleasant, so in an unspoken agreement, we scheduled them further and further apart. Strangely, it wasn't just Noah's doing. I actually thought he would drag his ass to their house more often if I asked him to. But I didn't ask.

The truth was I was getting tired of pretending that the most important part of my life didn't exist. I hadn't ever talked to my parents about Micah. They shut down any conversation related to me being gay, so mentioning my boyfriend simply hadn't been an option. That made it impossible to talk about a baseball game I had seen with Micah, or a good restaurant we had discovered, or most things I did outside of work, because I spent my free time with him.

The fact was a life couldn't be bifurcated that way and still shared. So I didn't share, and as a result, my relationship with my parents now felt less like a relationship and more like an obligation. I wasn't happy about any of that. I wished we could be close again. But there was no way for me to bridge the gap on my own.

"Yes, I'm moving. I'm sorry I didn't call you, Dad." I took a deep breath and prepared myself for an unpleasant reaction. "I'm moving in with my boyfriend. His name is—"

My mother covered her mouth with her hand as if this was horrifying information, and my father held his hand in front of him in a "stop right now" motion.

"That's enough of that kind of talk, Ben. You know how your mother and I feel about your unfortunate lifestyle choice, and yet you insist on throwing it in our faces."

I sighed and dragged my fingers through my hair. Saying I had a boyfriend constituted throwing it in their faces? "I'm sorry you're unhappy with the way I'm living my life. But it's my life, and there's nothing unfortunate about it. I'm a good man. Micah, that's my boyfriend, is a good man."

My mother came over to me and gave me a loose hug. "Of course you're a good man, Ben. But these things you're doing with other men aren't good. Please stop this, honey."

Got any advice for me here, folks? Because I was plumb out of ideas on how to talk to my parents. No? Okay, well, if at first you don't succeed...

"By *things*, I assume you're referring to sex." Those words made my mother gasp and step back. Sex was most certainly not an appropriate topic of conversation. But frankly, I thought we had left appropriate about three months back, or maybe it was three decades, but who's counting? "I wish you wouldn't marginalize my relationship that way. I'm in love with him, Mom. We're building a life together, a happy life. If you decide you want to be a part of it, please let me know. We'll have you over. And we're living just a few blocks away from Noah and Clark, so I'm sure they can join us. But right now, I need to get some more packing done before Micah gets here with dinner. Unless you want to meet him, in which case I can call and have him bring more food."

Needless to say my parents didn't want to meet Micah. So they left, and I got back to packing. But I didn't have quite the same spring in my step.

MICAH CALLED while I was packing pictures. And by packing, I mean I was looking at photos of my family back when my parents liked me, trying not to cry, and failing more frequently than I was willing to admit.

"Hi, honey. Listen, I think I must have gone too far or something. I'm almost at the Grant Boulevard exit," he said.

Yeah, I lived in the boonies. Well, it was the megachain, box store, cookie-cutter-subdivisions, suburbia version of the boonies.

"Sadly, no, that isn't too far. In fact, our town motto here in EC North is 'if you think you've gone too far, keep going a little longer and eventually you'll get here.' You've got three more exits and then you can get off the highway. I'm only about ten minutes from there."

Micah was in full-on traffic tension mode when he finally got to my condo. "Damn, Ben, I don't know how you've lived out here and made that drive every day for so long. I guess I've been out of LA long enough to have forgotten how much I hate being stuck in traffic. On the plus side, though, I learned a lot about people's political affiliations, personal causes, and the number of pets and children they have. How did we ever find out random and unnecessary trivia about people we don't know before bumper stickers? Oh, and what's the deal with the cartoon kid pissing on the different truck brands? Is there some sort of turf war going between Ford and Chevy? And where does that leave Dodge?"

All that came out in one fast rant, and then Micah looked closely at my face and his entire demeanor changed. He set the bag of takeout on the table and walked up to me, circling one arm around my waist and the other around the back of my head, threading his fingers through my hair. "What's the matter, honey? You don't look so good."

I snorted out a humorless laugh. "Thanks a lot."

The hand on my waist dropped to my ass and stroked

me gently, not trying to arouse, just to calm. "Come on. You know what I mean. You're still my pretty boy, but I can tell you're down and that you've been crying. Talk to me."

I dropped my forehead onto his shoulder and let him hold me up, physically and otherwise. "My parents stopped by. It feels like they'll never get past this. They can barely look at me, we can't talk about anything. We used to be close. I mean, they didn't really know me, so I guess we weren't actually close, but in a lot of ways we were... I'm not making any sense."

Micah kissed the side of my head. "You're making perfect sense. And you're doing everything possible to stay available and open to them when they finally realize you're still the same son they love and they want to have a good relationship with you again."

I tilted my head and pressed my face into Micah's neck, nuzzling his warm skin. "What if they never want that?" I asked.

"They will, honey, they will. It's just taking them a long time to get there."

"You promise?" My voice cracked and I sounded like a pathetic kid, but I so needed to know that someday I would be reconnected with my family.

"Aww, honey, I wish I could make you that promise, but I can't. What I can promise you is that you're not alone and you never will be. You have your brother and Clark. And you have me. I'm here, Ben, and I want to be your family too."

I tried to blink back tears, but I was pretty sure I failed. Again. "You're already my family. And you're my future." I raised my head and kissed him, just a tender meeting of our lips to show him how much he meant to me. "I love you, Micah."

CHAPTER TWENTY-THREE

"BEN FORMAN. With a name like that, I'm sure your ancestors must be Jewish. How much do you know about them?"

Ooookay, that one came out of left field. It was absolutely not on my list of possible introductory sentences or questions from Micah's mother. I had been prepared for repulsion along the same lines as my parents (even though Micah had repeatedly assured me that his parents had no issue whatsoever with his sexual orientation). I had been prepared for anger that I had moved into Micah's house without her ever having met me (even though Micah was certain all anger would be directed squarely at him). I had even been prepared for her to think I wasn't good enough for her son just because, well, I wasn't (Micah doesn't know about that particular fear. It was too pathetic for me to share, so please keep it to yourself). But comments about my religious heritage right off the bat? Uh, yeah, not so much on my overly thought and stressed-about what-will-happen-when-I-meet-Micah's-family list.

I stood paralyzed in the entryway of his parents' house with a suitcase in my left hand and my right hand about a quarter of the way up toward a handshake. I hadn't made it to a full extension before Micah's mother had thrown her question at me, and after that...like I said, paralyzed.

"Mom, come on! That question has been asked and answered. Three times. I told you on the phone already, Ben's family is Christian. Let. It. Go."

She rolled her eyes at Micah and then took a couple of steps toward me before nudging my hand aside and giving me a tight hug. "Are your grandparents still alive, dear?" she asked while giving me a warm embrace that was completely incongruous with her debilitating interrogation.

"Mom! Seriously, stop it."

She ignored Micah completely. "Or maybe you can ask your parents."

That seemed to be the last straw for Micah. He put his hands on her shoulders and turned her around so she was facing him. "So help me, Mother, one more question about Ben's family and we're staying in a hotel."

She managed to sound genuinely surprised and sincere when she said, "Did I say something wrong, Micah? I'm so sorry. I had no idea. It must be because I got so little sleep last night getting everything ready for your visit. I've been cooking practically nonstop for two days. I have a brisket ready for dinner, and I even made your Bubbe's sour cream coffee cake so you'd have something to eat after your flight. Ben might be hungry too. Is it okay if I offer him some cake and coffee, or is that offensive too? I wouldn't want to upset you, dear."

"Dad!" Micah shouted. "Dad, we're here!"

Was he planning to just ignore her question? The interaction was completely foreign to me. In my parents' house, things had always been cordial and nonconfrontational. Well, not including my recent coming out debacle. Oh, and any conversation involving Noah since about the age of twelve. But other than that...

"Micah!" An older version of Micah walked into the room and smiled broadly at his son, giving him a quick hug. Then he walked over to me and opened his arms. "And you must be Ben. We've heard so much about you. We're so glad you're here." He put his arm around my shoulders and guided me into the living room. "Micah tells me you do corporate work, a lot of M and A. I do the same thing on the real estate side. I bet we can share some good war stories."

I knew Micah's father was an attorney, but Micah hadn't ever mentioned his particular practice area. I was about to respond to his greeting when I became distracted by Micah's mother once again. She was talking to Micah in what I think was supposed to be a whisper but really wasn't.

"So tell me this, is he circumcised?"

That was it. I was scarred for life.

"Are you fucking kidding me right now, Mom? Did you seriously just ask me about my partner's penis?"

I wasn't sure which was more shocking, the fact that Micah's mother had made a reference to my dick or the fact that Micah had just said "fuck" in front of his parents.

His father apparently considered both things to be nonevents, because he just kept right on talking about work. "Just last week, I closed a three-party deal that was really fascinating. We drew up a PSA, a lease-back agreement, and..."

Should I tell Micah's mother that I was, in fact, cut? I mean, if it mattered that much to her... Holy crap, I was actually giving serious consideration to describing my dick to a sixty-something-year-old woman. Of course, I wasn't just volunteering the information out of thin air. I mean, said woman had been asking about my dick. Wait, did that actually matter, or was it a distinction without a difference? And was I seriously having this internal debate? Yeah, sadly, I was.

Tell me the truth, nothing's gonna be normal ever again, is it?

"ALL RIGHT, so if you want, I can create a distraction and you can make a run for the rental car. Give me like two minutes, and if I don't make it out there, just gun it and save yourself," Micah said.

We had just walked into the guest room to unpack after spending about thirty comparatively uneventful minutes eating a delicious cake, drinking tea, and chatting with his parents. I draped my arms over Micah's shoulders and leaned in for a kiss and a nibble on his lips.

"Are you kidding me? There's no way we're leaving. When else am I ever going to have the opportunity to see the unflappable Micah Trains completely unravel? Your mother is fiercely skilled. Do you think she'd mind if I videotaped this visit? We can show it to young associates as a CLE in deposing adverse witnesses."

He chuckled. "Where do you think I picked up my greatest tricks? But lest you think my mother can undo me, just wait and see. The student has outgrown the teacher, and I've figured out how to beat my mother at her own game. If she wants to know so much about your dick, I'll make sure to be extra loud tonight when I sing its praises." He got an evil glint in his eyes. "Come to think of it, why wait until tonight? I can take care of this right now."

He jogged over to the bed and threw himself down on it, making it squeak loudly. "Oh, Ben, yeah!" he shouted.

My eyes widened in horror, and I hissed at him, "Micah! What in the hell are you doing?"

He winked and kept bouncing as he yelled. "Harder, Ben, harder. Pound that big, hard, *circumcised* dick into me. Oh, yeah!"

Life doesn't do much to prepare you for watching your boyfriend put on a sex show for his parents, even if it is just auditory. But this was actually happening. Like for real. Swear to God. The Jason meets Freddy movie was less horrifying.

There was a knock on the door right before it swung open. I jerked my head over, ready to see angry parents, and instead there was a pretty brunette standing there with a sardonic grin on her face.

"Wow, Micah. If he can work you up that much without taking his pants off, I can't wait to see what his big, hard, circumcised dick can do when he actually sets it loose." And the parade of horrors continued. "In fact, I'm sure my children are wondering the same thing. I believe I'll help Ben unpack and get to know him a little better while you go out there and explain to Isaiah what exactly it means to pound your dick. Thanks for saving me the uncomfortable sex talk, Uncle Micah."

My face must have shown my mortification, because Micah's sister took my hand and smiled at me. "I'm just playing around. The kids are in the kitchen with their grandmother. They didn't hear a thing. I'm Sarah, by the way." She looked me up and down before continuing. "You know, you're even more gorgeous in person than you are in the pictures Micah e-mailed. What on earth are you doing with a troll like my brother?"

Micah jumped off the bed, marched over, and flipped Sarah onto his shoulder in a fireman's carry. "Buzz off, squirt. If Ben hasn't figured out that he's out of my league yet, then I don't need you pointing out the obvious."

"Micah, put me down! I'm not a kid anymore, Micah, I'm thirty-two years old. Seriously, put me down!"

He ignored his sister and looked at me. "Want to meet the greatest almost-six-year-old on the planet and his adorable baby sister?"

It turned out that Micah's nephew was able to broker a release of his mother. It wasn't so much because the boy was concerned about her well-being. More like he wanted to take her spot. So Micah dumped Sarah on the geometrically-patterned sectional couch and then lifted Isaiah onto his shoulders and started running around the house, making the kid giggle madly.

We heard a baby crying, so Sarah leapt off the couch and ran into the kitchen. She came back a few moments later with a sniffling baby. "Adina needs her binky." Her eyes darted around the room and landed on the diaper bag. She put the baby, who'd begun crying again, on one hip and bent over the bag, shuffling through it.

"You want me to take her while you do that? Seems like you have your hands full there."

She looked up at me gratefully and handed over the baby. "Would you? Thanks."

I held Adina against my chest and walked around the room, bouncing a little as I went and patting her back. She must have liked it, because she stopped crying and even rested her little head against my shoulder. I melted just a tiny bit. Okay, maybe more like a lot.

"Darn it! I think I forgot to pack a binky. I might have an extra one in the car." Sarah looked up from her diaper bag search, and her eyes warmed when she saw me. "You're great with her. Adina normally doesn't let anybody except for me and occasionally my mom hold her. Even Gabe, my husband, can't get her to settle when she's already in one of her moods."

I blushed at the compliment and dipped my face, inhaling Adina's sweet baby scent. "Thanks. She's adorable."

Sarah smiled and set the diaper bag back down on the floor. "I'll be right back. She seems fine now, but she could fall apart in a heartbeat. I better track down a binky or ask Gabe to stop by the house after work instead of coming straight here."

The baby was asleep in my arms by the time Sarah came back with two pacifiers in her hand. I couldn't tell whether she was happy or sad, because she was smiling, but her eyes were decidedly wet when she gazed at me holding her daughter. "Be right back." She cleared her throat. "I just need to clean these off; they were buried underneath the seat."

Forty minutes later, I was sitting on the couch, holding a still-sleeping Adina and getting to know Micah's sister and his parents while he played any number of games with his nephew. I think they were on hide-and-seek when Micah's mother got back to her earlier interrogation.

"So when Micah says your family is Christian, what does that mean exactly?"

I wasn't sure how he heard her over his own voice,

but Micah stopped counting in the middle of the word "six" and sped over. "Mom, we already talked about this. What's your obsession with Ben's religion? Seriously!"

"It's not an obsession, Micah. I'm just curious. It's important for us to carry on our traditions, and I worry that in an inter-faith household the children will end up falling away from Judaism because Christianity is so much more prevalent in our society. It's easy to become enamored by Christmas trees and Easter eggs. I'm sorry if your heritage means so little to you."

Micah's shoulders hunched and his hands flew up. "What children are we talking about here, Mom?"

She answered him in a very slow cadence, like he was having trouble understanding her words rather than her meaning. "We're talking about your children, Micah. Yours and Ben's. You did call me and say you were bringing home the young man you'd be spending your life with, right?" She nudged her head toward me. "I gather this is him, seeing as how you've told me that you're living together."

I was momentarily distracted from the odd conversation by that little anecdote. I loved that he told his parents about me, loved that he said we would be spending our lives together, loved him.

"Yeah, I said that. But Mom, you do realize we didn't move in together because either of us is knocked up, right? You get that it's not biologically possible, no matter how hard we try?"

His mother scowled at him. "Don't get fresh with me, Micah Trains. You can adopt or get a surrogate. Erma Stein's neighbor and his husband just did that very thing."

Micah looked at his father imploringly. "Dad? A little help here, please."

The man barely concealed a smirk. "Oh, I assure you, son, it's perfectly legal."

Honestly, I had never seen Micah so frazzled. It was even better than when his mother had asked about my dick. He collapsed onto the couch next to me, causing my body to shift in a way that jostled the baby. I immediately pressed my face to her ear and made a soft "shhhh" sound. She settled back down easily.

The same couldn't be said for Micah. "I know it's legal, that's not the issue," he responded to his father in an agitated tone.

"If you're worried about where to get an egg, I'm happy to donate mine," Sarah said. "You'll definitely want to make sure Ben's looks get handed down, so he should contribute the sperm. Otherwise, the kids might get teased at school."

It seemed as if Micah just gave up on his family at that point. He turned to me and kissed my cheek before smiling apologetically and whispering, "I'm sorry about this. For some reason, they've all chosen today to lose their ever-loving minds. Do you think we can get all three of them involuntarily committed at the same time, or would a judge frown on that?"

I winked at Sarah before shrugging and looking into Micah's eyes. "No reason to apologize to me. I agree with them completely. Surrogacy sounds like a great idea."

And with that, I rendered my always eloquent boyfriend completely speechless.

CHAPTER TWENTY-FOUR

I THINK the only thing I heard Micah say over the next three hours was, "Can you please pass the salt?"

By the time we got back into the guest room for the night, I was a little worried that we had all pushed him too far. He was leaning down, untying his laces, when I stepped up behind him and rubbed his back. "You okay?"

He straightened up, toed off his shoes, and then turned around. I stepped closer, and he embraced me, dropping his forehead against mine. "Yeah, I'm okay. I've just been thinking." He took a deep breath. "Listen, Ben, did you mean what you said out there, or were you just joining in with my family to take the piss?"

"I meant it."

He pulled his head back and searched my eyes. "You really want kids?"

Why was that so strange? Didn't everyone want to have a family? "Sure I do. I like kids. Don't you? You seem to get along great with your nephew."

He nodded. "Yeah, I like kids. I guess I just never thought of having any of my own. It never seemed, I don't know, possible or something."

I cupped Micah's face in my hands and stroked his beard with my thumbs. "It is possible. I like the idea of hiring a surrogate. The question is, do you want it? Not right away, I mean. We should enjoy some time with just each other first. But eventually, do you want to have kids?"

He was quiet for a long time, but his eyes never left my face. Eventually, he turned his lips into my hand and kissed my palm, before gazing back at me. When he spoke, his voice was a hoarse whisper.

"With you? Yeah, I think I do."

THE REST of our time with Micah's family was just as chaotic, loud, and intrusive as that first night. And I loved every single minute of it.

Both of his parents, but especially his mother, were exceptionally warm. Unlike my family, which rarely displayed physical affection, Micah's family was all about hugs and touches. And although Deborah, Micah's mom, meddled at an Olympic level, it was clear to me that she did it out of love for him. I was pretty sure Micah knew that too, despite his resolute refusal to acknowledge it. I even think the emotional chess game they played with each other was secretly fun for him. I sure knew that I enjoyed watching it, once the surgical history of my dick was no longer one of the pawns.

And celebrating their holidays with them was a wonderful experience too. I enjoyed learning about their traditions and was surprised by the deep sense of community they had with other members of their synagogue. It was like an extended family in a lot of ways. And not one person blinked an eye when I was introduced as Micah's partner, which was completely different from my experience with religion. I enjoyed it immensely.

One night, we were up late with Micah's parents. They were reminiscing about his growing up years and sharing childhood stories about Micah. I was soaking it all in, enjoying learning new things about a man I already felt I knew better than anyone.

They'd just finished telling me about a trip to Yosemite they took when Micah was in middle school. They'd lined the back of their station wagon with blankets and pillows, and the kids slept and played cards most of the way there. Deborah drank so much water that they turned their restroom stops into a game, collecting magnets from the different convenience stores lining the highway. And to that day, she had those magnets on her refrigerator and thought of her children at the ages they were back then whenever she looked at them.

When we got into bed that night, Micah was particularly loving. He snuggled up to me, wiggling his knee between my thighs, circling his arm around my waist, and nuzzling and kissing my neck and face.

"When you said we should wait to have kids, you didn't mean like a really long time, right? Because it'll probably take a while to find a surrogate and work out the contracts and stuff. Plus, they don't always get pregnant the first time. And then the pregnancy itself is nine months."

I traced his brow and jawline, ran my fingers over his prominent nose and soft beard, and gazed into intelligent blue eyes tinged with anticipation. Micah was so sexy. My dick filled and lengthened, causing an almost instantaneous reciprocal reaction in Micah's cock, which was pressed against my belly. "Umm, I hadn't thought about timing, but no, we don't have to wait a long time. What do you have in mind?"

He shrugged and found some way to burrow even closer to me. "Don't know. I'm just really excited about it. Talking about all those stories from growing up made me think about what it would be like for us to do the same stuff, you know? Car trips, Disneyland, birthday parties…"

I found Micah's mouth and kissed him, taking it deep from the start. Knowing he was thinking about those things, about us sharing our life that way, cranked me right up. "You'd be really good at teaching our kids how to blow that shofar thing from Rosh Hashana," I whispered when we finally broke for air. "Nobody can blow like you."

He laughed. "I can't believe straitlaced Benjamin Forman just turned a solemn religious tradition into a sexual reference."

I blushed. "I can't help it. When you had your lips around that horn, I was instantly hard. I had to strategically place the prayer book on my lap so your parents wouldn't notice."

He cracked up. "Oh, now you're bringing the siddur into it! I'm pretty sure you're mocking my culture and religion. Should I get my mom in here? I think she's ready to disown me and adopt you instead, but if she hears about this, I may still have a chance."

I rolled him onto his back and straddled his hips, planting my hands on either side of his head. "I'm not mocking anything. I admire your culture. Seriously, I think it's great. I've enjoyed learning about it from your parents. Why do you think I keep asking all those questions?"

Micah groaned and shifted underneath me. "Honey, if you actually expect me to engage in conversation right now, you've got to stop wiggling around on top of my dick. 'Cause at this moment, the only thing I can think about is doing my level best to prove biology wrong and breed you."

I clenched my ass reflexively in response to his comment. Being fucked sounded so good right then. Time to change the topic and test out my recently improved dirty talk skills. "Oh, yeah?" I dipped my head and blew hot air against his neck and ear. "You wanna bury your hard cock inside me and fill me up with your seed?"

He flipped me over and ground his dick against me. "You make me nuts. Completely fuckin' nuts. Do you have any idea how good you looked in your suit at temple? Or what you do to my stomach when I see you holding my niece? I've spent most of my waking hours on this trip holding myself back from molesting you in front of my family."

"Well, your family's not here now. Time to step up to the plate and show me what you've got."

Micah grinned and then leaned over to get the lube out of the bag we kept next to the bed. We had learned early on in our stay to be careful about what we left out because Deborah made a habit of going into the guest room to clean and change the sheets. I thought I was going to die when we walked in after an afternoon of shopping and found the bottle of lube on top of a coaster and our underwear washed and folded on the bed.

We were both too worked up for a lot of foreplay, so Micah's slick finger was circling my rosebud and pressing into my channel right away. His mouth met mine for another kiss, and I let my knees drop open, enjoying the feeling of him playing with my body. One finger turned into two, and then he corkscrewed and scissored them inside me.

"Nnnn. 'S good," I moaned before licking his lips and teasing out his tongue.

"You ready for me, honey?" he asked huskily.

"Uh-huh."

He settled between my knees and draped my legs over his shoulders, holding them in place with his forearm as he lined his slicked cock up with my hole. One firm push and his hard dick was inside, stretching me to my limit and making me cry out his name in pleasure. Micah kept his strokes steady, rubbing his cockhead over my gland as he pushed in and then circled his hips before pulling back out again.

I looked at his wiry body kneeling between my thighs, holding onto my knees as he bent me in half and pounded into me. A sheen of sweat covered his face and chest, the veins in his neck bulged, and he grunted every time he bottomed out. Damn, was he ever sexy.

When it looked like he was close to finishing, I reached for my cock.

"Don't," he rasped as he shook his head. "That's mine and I have plans for it."

I dropped my arm and let him drive, enjoying his body warmth and tightening my muscles around his dick on every out-stroke.

"Fuck, that feels good. I'm almost there, Ben. Gonna fill you up." His rhythm changed, the pushes coming faster and getting harder before he held himself deep inside and stiffened. "Yes, yes, yes!"

I could feel his cock pulsing inside me, and I almost whimpered in frustration, wanting so much to join him in ecstasy. It only took a few moments before he let out a deep breath and pulled his softening dick out of my ass. He lowered my legs and bent down, licking my dick from base to tip before taking it into his mouth and sucking hard while he rolled my balls in his hand.

"Yeah, Micah. Like that." Just when I could feel my orgasm pooling at the base of my spine, he popped off my dick. "No, don't stop," I whined. "Wanna come so bad, Micah."

"Don't worry, honey, I won't leave you hanging." His finger dipped into my crease and circled my hole, making me tremble. "You sore?"

"Just a little. I like it, though. Please, Micah." I didn't care how desperate I sounded.

He kissed my inner thigh, then my balls, and then his hands clasped my cheeks and pull them open, leaving my freshly fucked opening completely exposed. Before I could think about what he was doing, Micah's tongue was there, lapping at the puckered skin, rimming my hole, and then darting inside.

"Oh my God! What are you doing?"

He pulled his tongue out of my body and took a long swipe up my valley. "Tasting myself inside of you."

I whimpered and almost came right then. Micah lowered his face and got back to his task, working my ass over with his mouth, licking me, swiping that wet muscle inside me, and generally driving me insane. My brain was overwhelmed with pleasure as I started rocking my hips, humping his face and begging for more.

Micah gave me exactly what I needed, not stopping, not slowing, just eating me out with unmatched fervor. Then he took my dick into his hand and gave it a few strokes and

I was biting my fist to keep from shouting loud enough to wake his parents as a killer orgasm racked my body.

"Aww, geez, that was incredible, Micah," I gasped out. "I can't believe you did that."

I looked down and saw him gazing at me while he brought his hand to his mouth and licked my release off his palm before stretching his fingers out and running his tongue on the webbing of cum between them, trying to get every last drop.

"You're the sexiest thing I've ever seen, and I'm pretty sure you're going to kill me," I said.

He stretched his body on top of mine and smiled down at me. "You're not allowed to die, honey. We're going to make babies together, remember?"

"Right now, I'm not sure I remember my own name."

"Benjamin. Isaac. Forman." He placed a kiss on my lips after each word. "The love of my life."

I chuckled. "Do you have any idea how cheesy you are?"

He shrugged. "Hey, great sex will do that. Melts my body and scrambles my brain."

Well, I couldn't argue with that logic. The sex was great. Come to think of it, other than the situation with my parents, my entire life was pretty great.

CHAPTER TWENTY-FIVE

THE NEXT year flew by, despite being very busy. Micah stayed true to his word and managed to ratchet his schedule down to something in the range of normal. And even though he gave his mother a hard time about nagging us and claimed to have never considered having children of his own, he did endless research about surrogacy and took the lead in working out the paperwork.

For some reason, he got it into his head that we had to have a baby before he turned forty. Don't ask me where he came up with the idea or how it made any sort of sense, but I wasn't going to argue with him. I was ready for us to expand our little family.

Sarah and Gabe came out to Emile City when it was time to harvest the eggs. They brought both kids and made a vacation out of it. We all had a great time.

Being pumped up on hormones hadn't been easy for Sarah, so we made her spa appointments and let her relax while Micah, Gabe, and I took the kids out on the town. Turned out we had a children's museum in Emile City that had a range of activities wide enough to keep both Adina and Isaiah entertained. The science museum was another favorite for Isaiah, and I spent most of my time finding ways to keep Adina occupied. And when all else failed, we hit the park and spent an afternoon swinging and sliding. Micah and I considered it a snapshot of our future, and we liked what we saw.

Even the trip to the clinic was fun. Well, it was fun for Micah and me, but according to Sarah, the egg harvesting experience wasn't as enjoyable as the method we used to remove my portion of the donation. It was so enjoyable, in fact, that I refused to feel embarrassed about the knowing grins we got from the nurses when we came out of the little room after filling the plastic jar.

But none of that held a candle to how happy we were a few weeks later when we got a call telling us the pregnancy test was positive. We were nine months away from being fathers.

I managed not to worry as much about my parents because everything else in my life was going so well. But my relationship with them continued to be strained. They refused to acknowledge Micah, which meant that if I wanted to see them, I had to go to their house. I had a lot going on, not that I could tell them about any of it, so I didn't see them often. And when I did, it was still incredibly frustrating, still disappointing, and still made my heart hurt a little. But I kept trying, even though I had reached a point where I no longer believed anything would ever change between us.

ONE OF the things that had been taking up my time since Micah and I had returned from that trip to visit his family was meeting with Rabbi Seth. I didn't want Micah to know about it, so I had scheduled our meetings during the workday, and I had been surprisingly successful in keeping him in the dark. My man had incredible focus while he was working, which I found to be a major turn-on.

"I was hoping we could stay in tonight and rent a movie or something, but Seth's been all over me the last few days about coming to temple," Micah said as we drove home from work on a Friday evening. I curled my lips in to hold down my knowing grin. "I don't know what his damage is all of a sudden, 'cause he's not usually pushy. But it probably has been too long since I've been, so I agreed."

"It's no problem," I said, making sure to keep my voice even. "I'll come with you."

He swung his head toward me. "Really? You want to come to temple?"

I shrugged nonchalantly. "Sure, could be fun."

MY HANDS trembled a bit with nerves as I got dressed, but mostly I was excited. Micah introduced me to a few people when we got there, and then we found Eli, who gave me a tight hug and leaned in close as he whispered, "Glad to have you as a member of the tribe."

It felt like time jumped after that, and suddenly Seth was doing the Torah reading. I straightened my tie and waited my turn.

"Ben Forman, would you please join me on the bima?" Seth said.

Micah's eyes widened, and he grabbed my hand. "What's going on?"

I raised our joined hands to my mouth and kissed his. Then I let go and joined Seth in front of the congregation.

"Many of you know Micah Trains, but you might not know his partner, Ben Forman. Last fall, Ben called me and said he wanted to learn more about Judaism. When I asked him why, he said that he'd spent the high holidays with Micah's family and he'd enjoyed the ritual and the sense of community he'd experienced, so he wanted to learn more about his partner's heritage."

I looked over at Micah, wanting to see his reaction. His eyes were wide, his face a little flushed. I refocused on Rabbi Seth.

"So we met a few times, I recommended some books, and then, a few weeks later, I got another call from Ben. This time he said he wanted to convert. I turned him away at first, but Ben was persistent. So the third time he asked, I raised the same question. Why? Ben explained that he and Micah were going to start a family and he wanted to help pass down our culture and beliefs to their children. And since they were one family, Ben felt it was important for him to share in those things, which meant becoming Jewish. So I agreed. And after a year of meetings and lessons, tonight, I'm thrilled to welcome Ben into our community."

Another quick glance at Micah showed me how deeply this was affecting him. His eyes were wet with unshed tears, and he had the most beautiful smile on his face. Then our gazes met and his lips moved, miming the words, "I love you."

I knew that, of course. I could tell from every look and every touch. And I felt the same way about him.

ONE OF the unexpected things about having children is how much gear is involved. And by the way, the plural on that was intentional—*children*. As in twins. A boy and a girl. "Excited" didn't even begin to cover how Micah and I felt when we sat in the ultrasound room and heard that news.

Our friend Caleb was a designer, and he volunteered to help us decorate the babies' room. I was actually surprised at how much modern baby furniture he was able to find. It fit perfectly in our house. So before we knew it, we had high chairs that looked a little like space pods, one in green and one in orange. We had espresso-stained cribs in a room painted a bright yellow color with a blue, cloudy mural on the ceiling. We had drawers overflowing with tiny too-cute-for-words clothing and soft blankets. And both of our cars had baby seats installed in the back.

Supply-wise we were totally ready to go, but that didn't stop me from being a nervous wreck the day we went to the hospital. Micah called his parents and sister to tell them Raphael and Lilah had finally arrived. And I called Noah and Clark to let them know they were uncles.

"Congratulations, Ben. I'm happy for you, man, really happy for you. We'll come by the hospital to meet our niece and nephew tonight. Send me a text and let me know what you want to eat, and we'll bring you and Micah dinner."

I was holding a little angel swaddled in a blue and pink striped blanket, so it was hard to focus on anything else, but I was pretty sure I managed to stammer out a "Sounds good. Thanks, Noah."

"Oh, Ben, one more thing," Noah said.

"Uh-huh?"

"I assume you haven't told Mom and Dad about your babies. Do you want me to call them to let them know?"

Well, wasn't that a fine question? I hadn't told my parents we were expecting, so hearing they were suddenly grandparents would probably throw them for a loop. But you know what? That wasn't my problem. I would have loved the opportunity to share my good news with them. Hell, I would have loved the opportunity to share all sorts of things with them, but they'd insistently shut themselves off from most of my life.

"I hate to ask you to face the firing squad that way, Noah. But if you're willing to do it, I'd really appreciate it."

"No problem. You don't need to let their bullshit get in your way. Go enjoy your kids. Oh, and Clark says to tell Micah he owes him big time."

"Owes him for what?" I asked.

I heard Clark's voice in the background, then a shuffle like the phone was changing hands before Clark came on the line. "I owe him for bringing my friend back. I missed you for all those years, Ben, and I'm really glad we're back in each other's lives again." He cleared his throat and then continued. "Now go tell my niece and nephew that Uncle Clark and Uncle Noah are coming over later with the first of what I'm sure will be a lifetime supply of overindulgent presents."

Noah and Clark did come to the hospital that evening. They brought us dinner, held the babies, and chatted for a little while, and then the two of them went home.

The next evening, Micah and I went home too, but it was no longer just the two of us. We had planned to take turns feeding the babies during the night, but neither of us managed to stay in bed. Thankfully the glider chairs Caleb had picked out for the nursery were comfortable, because we spent more time in them than in our own room the first night.

A FEW mostly sleepless nights in a row meant I was sleeping when the doorbell rang at ten in the morning. Actually, I didn't even hear it ring, so I didn't know the exact time. But that was the hour when the sound of my father's voice woke me. It was so out of left field that I shot up in bed, certain it had been a dream. But then I heard my mother's muffled voice too.

I rubbed my eyes and tried to get my bearings. What on earth were my parents doing at our house? Oh, God, Micah was stuck alone with them.

I jumped out of bed and yanked on a T-shirt before rushing out of the bedroom and into the living room. The sight that greeted me brought me to a halt.

My mother and father were sitting on my couch, holding my children and talking with my partner. And all of them looked happy.

"Mom? Dad?" my voice cracked.

Micah got up and reached his hand out to me. I walked to his side and stood close, needing his strength and wanting him to know that he had mine. He draped his arm around my shoulders, and his hand found its usual spot on the back of my head, fingers curling into my hair. I saw both of my parents' eyes follow the movement and blink in surprise. But they didn't say anything about it or storm out.

"We're sorry to wake you, son. We remember how valuable sleep can be during these first few months," my father said.

My mother looked up at me and wiped tears away with the hand that wasn't supporting Lilah. "Your children are just beautiful, Ben. I think Lilah favors you and Raphael favors your, umm..." She looked at Micah questioningly.

"Partner is fine, Mrs. Forman."

She nodded. "Thank you. And please, call me Gloria."

Micah nodded. Then he looked at me carefully, as if evaluating my emotional condition. I was still upright, which I figured should go in the win column.

"Are you thirsty, honey? Why don't you sit and catch up with your parents while I get us something to drink." I nodded dumbly, still trying to wrap my brain around what was happening. Micah looked at my parents. "What can I get for you to drink?"

"Water's fine for me and Byron, dear."

Micah was out of the room and back with four bottles of water before I managed to move from my spot. He handed a water bottle to each of my parents and then came over to me, leading us to the other sofa and staying close as we sat down. I leaned into him, needing to feel his solid strength. I was finally able to relax when he put his arm around me again.

"So, um, Micah," my father said, darting his eyes back

and forth between us. "What do you do for a living?"

Micah was apparently unbothered by my father's reaction to our affection, because his voice was steady as always when he answered. "I'm a lawyer. Commercial litigation. Ben and I actually work together. That's how we met."

And just like that, my parents and Micah started talking about his practice, about where he grew up, about his family. Once I got over the shock of their presence in my house, I joined in too. And suddenly, we were all talking. Really talking. Not fighting or exchanging passive-aggressive barbs. Talking.

The only possible explanation I could come up with for my parents' sudden change in attitude was the two beautiful babies they were holding. I had always known that having children would mean expanding my family, but I had no idea it would mean healing my family too. Yet somehow two little people who didn't know how to talk had managed to accomplish in one moment what I had failed to do in going on two years. They'd given me my parents back.

Oh, I realized it would take a while for us all to feel totally comfortable together. But it seemed as if my mom and dad were finally willing to try, which was good enough for me. After all, I had everything I had ever wanted.

I'VE HEARD so many gay friends say that we were born this way, that we had no choice in the matter. Well, that's true. But now? Well, now being gay means sharing my life and raising my children with a man I love. And that's a choice I would happily make over and over again.

THE END

(BUT WAIT…THERE'S MORE—BONUS CHAPTER AHEAD.)

BONUS CHAPTER

*When the U.S. Supreme Court released their historic marriage
decision, I wanted to celebrate so I wrote a bonus chapter with
Ben and Micah's reaction to the wonderful news. I hope you enjoy
it. –CC*

I PROBABLY should have seen it coming. It's not as if I live
under a rock. But I do sometimes get trapped under a pile
of laundry and a mountain of baby gear, each of which is a
hundred times the size of the babies who use them. Plus I
have a full-time job and an insatiable boyfriend. So with all
that in mind, you can understand how maybe I was distracted
enough not to predict the obvious.

"Morning, honey," Micah said as he walked into the
shower. I was rinsing my face, so my back was to him, but
just the sound of his gravelly voice was enough to make my
cock perk up and take notice.

He pressed his nude body to mine, his front against
my back, wrapped his left arm around my chest and his right
arm around my hip, and peppered the back of my neck with
kisses while he tweaked my nipple and groped my balls.

"Good morning." I leaned back against him and wiped
the water from my eyes. "Did you check on Raph and Lilah?"

"Yup." He nibbled his way to my ear and then sucked on my lobe. "They're still sleeping."

That was all I needed to hear. I covered his hand with mine and moved it to my dick, telling him without words what I wanted him to do. He chuckled but followed my lead, circling his long fingers around my cock right away.

"Get me the lube, Ben, and I'll make you feel good."

He moved his hand off my chest and held it out palm up. I grappled for the bottle and handed it to him. He kept fondling my dick with his right hand as he slowly moved his left hand down until it was in front of my groin. Then he opened the bottle and drizzled the slick onto my heated skin.

"Micah," I groaned and dropped my head back on his shoulder. "Love you."

A couple of strokes and then he scooted back for a few seconds. When his lubed cock pressed between my thighs, my breath hitched.

Damn, but did I ever love his dick. Loved how it felt in my hand, loved how it stretched my ass, loved how it tasted on my tongue. Seriously, whenever we were alone, I had to touch it, had to, even if it was nothing more than my hand down his pants while we were cuddling in front of the TV. It was like an obsession.

Micah sometimes teased me by saying I'd been dick-deprived because it took me so long to come out. I'd always point out that I was born with one of my own, so deprivation really wasn't the issue; I just thought he was sexy as hell and couldn't keep my hands off him. He usually stopped talking after that and did better things with his mouth.

"Love you too, honey," Micah said; then his warmth was back and we started moving in concert with one another.

I flattened my palms against the tile and rocked my hips. Micah pushed his dick between my thighs and up against my balls while he fisted my erection with sure, hard strokes. I closed my eyes and relished the connection we shared, how right it felt when we were together.

"God," I moaned as I started rocking faster and breathing harder. "I'm almost there already." He always did that to me—wound me up so quickly it was all I could do to hold my orgasm at bay in the face of his ministrations.

"Me too," he grunted into my ear. "Won't take me long."

After another few strokes of his skilled hand and a particularly well-placed nudge of his crown against my balls, I started shooting off and practically crying from the pleasure he gave me. I was still pulsing over Micah's fist when he shouted my name and coated me with his seed.

"Mmm," he sighed into my ear as he slowed his movements and caressed my hip and thigh. "That was nice."

I turned my head and kissed his bearded cheek. "Have I ever told you how much I love waking up with you?" I asked.

"Beats beating off alone, huh?" he asked dryly.

"Very funny."

One tight squeeze, a kiss on my shoulder, and then he pulled back and reached for the soap. "We better hurry; the twins are sure to wake up any second."

WE HAD become a well-oiled machine over the past nine months, which was key with two babies and two full-time jobs. Well, I had a full-time job. Although Micah worked way less than he ever had, he still racked up more hours than anyone could consider typical; forty hours a week just wasn't in his makeup.

The good news was he was crazy-focused, so he powered through more billable hours during the times we were at the office than I previously thought possible. We drove in together every day. Then I'd come to his office when I was done, and he'd shoulder his laptop and follow me to our car. After that, he'd usually manage to keep away from his computer until the kids and I were asleep.

When I'd wake up to find him typing away at three in the morning, I'd worry that he was still pushing himself too hard. But Micah assured me he was fine and that we had college savings accounts to worry about. My man was stubborn and he argued for a living, so I knew I wouldn't win a middle-of-the-night debate. Luckily, even after having seen me covered in baby vomit, he still found me irresistible, which meant walking naked into our home office and giving myself a few strokes was usually all it took to get him to follow me right back to bed.

Anyway, on the day I should have seen coming but didn't, we were neck-deep in the morning rush—Micah was feeding the twins and I was doing diaper duty—when he said, "Okay, I think Lilah is all done with her mush, and she's ready for you."

"It isn't mush," I answered as I unbuckled her from her orange high chair. "It's cereal."

Micah kissed our daughter's forehead and then mine before holding up his evidence. "Mush," he said, pointing at the bowl.

"The box calls it cereal," I countered, settling Lilah on my hip. We'd learned early on to get our kids fed and dressed before putting on our work clothes. Before that, the dry-cleaning bills had been astronomical.

Micah put the bowls and spoons in the sink and started wiping down the chairs and table. Raphi had an uncanny ability to spray cereal everywhere. "That's called creative marketing, honey."

"Whatever."

"That's your rebuttal?" He smirked. "I win."

I rolled my eyes. "You always win."

The cocky grin dropped from Micah's face, and he left the sponge on the table. I gulped when I saw a familiar gleam in his eyes.

"I feel like that every day, Ben," he said as he crowded

me up against the fridge and wrapped one hand around my shoulder and the other around my hip. He shifted his gaze from Raphi sitting on a play mat in the corner, to Lilah in my arms, and finally to me. Then he leaned forward and paused with his lips almost touching mine. "Feel like I won everything the day you agreed to be with me."

He kissed me then, light and sweet, but I was still grateful for his hands on me because I went weak in the knees.

"Hello!" our nanny, Laura, called out. "I'm here."

"We're in the kitchen, Laura," Micah responded.

"Are you decent?" she asked.

I blushed and Micah chuckled. "Cut it out. You're embarrassing Ben. Besides, it was one time, four months ago, and you didn't see all that much."

She came bustling in and took Lilah from me. "I'm an old woman," she said. "My heart can't take too much excitement. Now off with you both." She shooed us toward the door. "You go to work. It's my time with these babies." Then she looked around the kitchen and scowled. "It was clean in here when I left yesterday."

I shifted my gaze around our kitchen. There were a few dishes in the sink, and Micah hadn't quite finished wiping down the table, but otherwise, it looked clean. "Oh," I said nervously. "I'll, uh—"

"Never mind, I'll take care of it. Again." Laura shook her head. "Go on, now," she said.

Micah grinned and kissed Laura's cheek. He adored Laura, and no matter how often she criticized us or complained about something, he'd laugh it off. In fact, if I didn't know better, I'd say he enjoyed it.

I was pretty sure I saw her smile a bit as she walked over to the sink and started wiping cereal off Lilah's face. Then Micah took my hand and pulled me out of the room.

"Do you think she's upset about the kitchen?" I whispered to Micah once we were in our bedroom with the door shut and I knew nobody else could hear us. "'Cause it really isn't dirty."

He laughed and then froze with his slacks halfway up his thighs and looked up at me. "Wait, you're serious?"

I nodded as I stuffed my pajama pants and T-shirt into the hamper. "Well, yeah. You heard her."

"Oh, honey." He tilted the corner of his mouth up just a bit. "She doesn't mean anything by it," he explained. "And actually," he continued as he walked over to me, "I'm pretty sure she likes looking for things we've done wrong because then she can fix them."

"That doesn't make any sense."

"Sure it does. It makes her feel needed," he said as he pressed his bare chest against mine.

I felt my dick start to fill and darted my eyes toward the door. "Laura's in the other room," I hissed.

He kissed the tip of my nose. "The door is closed, and besides, I'm not seducing you."

I squeezed his hip and then forced myself to move away and start getting dressed. "It doesn't take much for you to seduce me and you know it," I said. I was thinking about what Micah had said about our nanny, which was distracting enough to slow me down, so he was done getting dressed before me.

"Here, let me help you," he said as he batted my hands away from my necktie. He straightened it and then started looping the fabric.

"Oh my God!" I said. "I just realized something."

"What?" he asked as he tightened the knot and then drew it up to my collar, leaving a perfect dimple at the top.

"Laura is pushy like your mother!" I shared my revelation excitedly.

Micah smirked and raised one eyebrow. He flattened and straightened my collar.

"Not that your mother is pushy," I added in a rush, realizing how bad that sounded.

Micah threw his head back and laughed. "You are so sweet, you know that?" He kissed my cheek again and then handed me my phone and my watch. "Yes, my mother is pushy. And, yes, it has occurred to me that Laura shares that particular personality trait."

I stuffed my phone in my pocket and clasped my watch over my wrist. "I can't decide if it's cute or sick that you not only know this, but like it enough to seek it out in the person who is helping us raise our children."

He paused with his hand on the doorknob and then shrugged as he opened it. "Yeah, I'm not sure either. Hey, I have some stuff to do out of the office today, so I won't be around, but I'll be back before it's time to go home."

"Okay." I followed him out of the room.

I HAD just finished up a conference call when Micah walked into my office. "You ready to go?" he asked.

I glanced at the clock on my computer. "It's only four o'clock," I said.

He shrugged. "I know, but I got done early, so I thought I'd check in to see if you were ready too." He tapped his foot rapidly. "If you have more to do, I can wait." He clenched his fists, cracked his knuckles, and tapped his foot even faster.

"Uh, no. I'm fine leaving now," I answered, wondering why Micah was twitchy. "Is everything okay?" I asked.

"Huh? Oh yeah, I'm fine."

I figured he was distracted by a case, so I didn't push him. Instead, when we got into the elevator, I took his hand in mine and rubbed my thumb over his wrist. He didn't say anything, but I thought some tension left his body.

We stayed quiet as we walked through the garage and climbed into our car. I turned on the radio, thinking some music would help Micah unwind. Eventually he'd talk to me about whatever he had on his mind. That was one of the things that had changed since I'd met Micah. Not the talking part—he was always good at that. But for most of my life, I had suffered from anxiety about all sorts of things, and seeing someone I cared about acting different or withdrawn would have sent me into a tailspin. I would have blamed myself, figured I'd done something wrong, and gotten depressed.

Don't I sound like a catch? Yeah, I never thought so either. So you can see why I still had to pinch myself sometimes about the fact that a man as steady, as smart, as confident as Micah Trains would want to build a life with me. And the most amazing thing about Micah was that he not only chose me, but he had an uncanny ability to make me feel like he thought *he* was the lucky one, like *I* was some sort of prize. Even better, the longer I lived with him, the more time we spent together, the more I felt like there had to be something pretty good about me, because I'd landed a man like him.

Anyway, that's all background to explain why it didn't once cross my mind that Micah's weird mood had anything to do with me. But then we pulled out of the garage and things started getting a little hinky.

"Uh, Micah?" I said when he turned in the opposite direction of our house. "Where're we going?"

"I have a stop to make," he said. His voice sounded a little shaky, which was totally out of character, but I left it alone.

"Don't be surprised if we start getting regular visits

from the UPS guy," I said, hoping to distract him from whatever had him so wound up.

Micah snorted. "Don't tell me. You bought more clothes for the kids."

"I was bored on a conference call today and I got an e-mail with the most adorable pink frilly stuff."

"Got it. More pink frilly things coming our way. And should I assume this also means we can expect more baby chinos and little itty-bitty baby polo shirts?"

His sarcastic tone was not lost on me. "I can't buy things for Lilah without getting things for Raph," I explained.

"Of course not. He'd be terribly wounded. I mean, they'll be one soon, after all. They're very sensitive at this age. And—" He paused and seemed to be swallowing down a laugh. "—also very preppy."

I looked at Micah and scowled. "I can't decide whether you're making fun of the types of clothes I buy or the volume. Just so you know, most of them were on sale. Plus they sent me a coupon. I saved us a ton of money."

"Yes." Micah nodded solemnly. "It's almost like they paid us to take the clothes off their hands."

"Cut it out," I said. I tried to keep up the scowl, but Micah was smiling, so it was impossible for me to even pretend I was angry. His happiness was always contagious.

"No, seriously," he continued. "Let me know if you get a coupon for a room addition, because with all the money we're making on the clothes you keep buying, we'll need to add on some giant closets pretty soon."

"Very funny. You should be thanking me for making sure the kids look..." I became distracted when we pulled up to the valet stand at the Golden Pine Inn. "What are we doing here?" I asked. "Are they a new client?"

Micah took in a deep breath and swallowed hard. "Nope," he said as he put the car in park and twisted his body until he was facing me. "Surprise!"

The valet opened his door.

"What's going on?" I asked, trying to catch up.

"Your brother and Clark are watching the kids tonight," Micah said. "And I got us a room here."

He got out of the car, and I followed him, taking his hand when he held it out to me. He led me through the lobby and into an elevator, and before long, he was slipping a keycard into a mahogany door.

"After you," he said as he held the door open.

I walked inside and gasped. The room was as gorgeous as I would have expected for the top boutique hotel in Emile City—antique furniture, silk linens, original artwork. But what I didn't expect, what I hadn't seen coming, were the rose petals on the bed and the scented candles on the nightstands.

"Micah, what's going on?" I asked as I turned around.

My always-confident boyfriend was down on one knee, holding a box in his trembling hand.

"Ben," he said, and then he rubbed his lips together

and took a deep breath. "I promised you flowers and candles and a romantic proposal just as soon as we could get married and have it mean something." He swallowed hard. "Well, you know they overturned DOMA yesterday. We still have a while before that'll make a difference on the state level here, but we can go to New York or DC or one of the other states where it's legal now, and then we'll at least have the federal rights. Plus, it's only a matter of time until—"

"Yes!" I shouted.

"Yes?" he repeated and stopped rambling about the legal ramifications of the Supreme Court decision to overturn the Defense of Marriage Act.

I dropped to my knees in front of him and draped my arms over his shoulders. "Well, technically, I think you have to ask me first," I teased.

He wrapped his arms around my waist and leaned his forehead against mine. "Ben Forman, will you keep making me the happiest guy on earth and marry me?"

It was the easiest question I had ever been asked. "Yes."

THE END

ABOUT THE AUTHOR

Cardeno C.—CC to friends—is a hopeless romantic who wants to add a lot of happiness and a few *awwws* into a reader's day. Writing is a nice break from real life as a corporate type and volunteer work with gay rights organizations. Cardeno's stories range from sweet to intense, contemporary to paranormal, long to short, but they always include strong relationships and walks into the happily-ever-after sunset.

Email: cardenoc@gmail.com

Website: www.cardenoc.com

Twitter: https://twitter.com/cardenoc

Facebook: http://www.facebook.com/CardenoC

Pinterest: http://www.pinterest.com/cardenoC

Blog: http://caferisque.blogspot.com

OTHER BOOKS BY CARDENO C.

SIPHON
Johnnie

HOPE
McFarland's Farm
Jesse's Diner

PACK
Blue Mountain
Red River

HOME
He Completes Me
Home Again
Just What the Truth Is
Love at First Sight
The One Who Saves Me
Where He Ends and I Begin
Walk With Me

FAMILY
The Half of Us
Something in the Way He Needs
Strong Enough
More Than Everything

MATES
In Your Eyes
Until Forever Comes
Wake Me Up Inside

FRIENDS
Not a Game

NOVELS
Strange Bedfellows
Perfect Imperfections
Control *(with Mary Calmes)*

NOVELLAS
A Shot at Forgiveness
All of Me
Places in Time
In Another Life & Eight Days
Jumping In

AVAILABLE NOW

He Completes Me
(2nd Edition)

Not even his mother's funeral can convince self-proclaimed party boy Zach Johnson to tone down his snark or think about settling down. He is who he is, and he refuses to change for anyone. When straight-laced, compassionate Aaron Paulson claims he's falling for him, Zach is certain Aaron sees him as another project, one more lost soul for the idealistic Aaron to save. But Zach doesn't need to be fixed and he refuses to be with someone who sees him as broken.

Patience is one of Aaron's many virtues. He has waited years for a man who can share his heart and complete his life and he insists Zach is the one. Pride, fear, and old hurts wither in the wake of Aaron's adoring loyalty and as Zach reevaluates his perceptions of love and family, he finds himself tempted to believe in the impossible: a happily-ever-after.

Home Again
(2nd Edition)

Imposing, temperamental Noah Forman wakes up in a hospital and can't remember how he got there. He holds it together, taking comfort in the fact that the man he has loved since childhood is on the way. But when his one and only finally arrives, Noah is horrified to discover that he doesn't remember anything from the past three years.

Loyal, serious Clark Lehman built a life around the person who insisted from their first meeting that they were meant to be together. Now, years later, two men whose love has never faltered must relive their most treasured and most painful moments in order to recover lost memories and secure their future.

Love at First Sight
(2nd Edition)

The moment naïve, optimistic Jonathan Doyle glimpses a gorgeous blue-eyed stranger from afar, he believes in love at first sight. Unfortunately, he loses sight of the man before they meet and then spends years desperately trying to find him. Just as he is about to give up, Jonathan gets a break and finally encounters David Miller face to face.

Successful, confident David turns Jonathan's previously lonely life into a fairy tale, giving him more than he ever imagined. But the years spent searching were hard on Jonathan, and he's terrified his young son and scandalous past will destroy his blossoming relationship. For David and Jonathan to build a future together, they'll both have to dig deep: David for the courage to share himself in a way he's never considered and Jonathan for the strength to tell the truth.

The One Who Saves Me
(2nd Edition)

At fourteen, Andrew Thompson and Caleb Lakes become best friends. As the years pass, they stand by each other through family trauma, school, and the start of their careers. They share their first sexual experiences, learning and experimenting, and they talk each other through countless dates and breakups.

Decades of trust and loyalty build a deep and abiding friendship, one that surpasses any relationship in their lives. But when the parameters of their unique friendship change, neither man knows how to break out of their established roles to build something new. After all, boyfriends come and go, but best friends are forever.

Where He Ends and I Begin
(2nd Edition)

Aggressive, physical, and brave, Jake Owens is a small town football hero turned big city cop who passes his time with meaningless encounters believing he can't have who he really wants: Nate Richardson, his best friend since before forever. Thoughtful, quiet, and kind, Nate is a brilliant doctor who has always known who he is and has never been able to shake his crush on loyal, courageous, *straight* Jake.

After a passionate night together, Nate realizes Jake isn't as straight as he assumed, but he worries that what they shared was a fluke, a result of too much closeness for too long. For Jake, the question isn't how they ended up in bed together because he has always known that Nate holds his heart, it's how he'll convince Nate that he wants and needs to stay there.

Walk With Me
(2nd Edition)

When Eli Block steps into his parents' living room and sees his childhood crush sitting on the couch, he starts a shameless campaign to seduce the young rabbi. Unfortunately, Seth Cohen barely remembers Eli and he resolutely shuts down all his advances. As a tenuous and then binding friendship forms between the two men, Eli must find a way to move past his unrequited love while still keeping his best friend in his life. Not an easy feat when the same person occupies both roles.

Professional, proper Seth is shocked by Eli's brashness, overt sexuality, and easy defiance of societal norms. But he's also drawn to the happy, funny, light-filled man. As their friendship deepens over the years, Seth watches Eli mature into a man he admires and respects. When Seth finds himself longing for what Eli had so easily offered, he has to decide whether he's willing to veer from his safe life-plan to build a future with Eli.

www.ingramcontent.com/pod-product-compliance
Lightning Source LLC
Chambersburg PA
CBHW070655180626
46817CB00006B/2386